JUL 1 0 2015

IMMUNITY

IMMUNITY

TAYLOR ANTRIM

Regan Arts.

NEW YORK

ALSO BY TAYLOR ANTRIM

The Headmaster Ritual

Regan Arts.
65 Bleecker Street
New York, NY 10012

Copyright © 2015 by Taylor Antrim

First Regan Arts hardcover edition, May 2015.

Library of Congress Control Number: 2014955524

ISBN 978-1-941393-28-4

Interior design by Nancy Singer
Jacket design by Richard Ljoenes

Printed in the United States of America

10 9 8 7 6 5 4 3 2 1

To Vivian

What's natural is the microbe.
All the rest—health, integrity, purity (if you
like)—is a product of the human will,
of a vigilance that must never falter.

—Albert Camus, *The Plague*

SICK

1

"You're Catherine," Mercer said, crossing the airy vault of the office.

Catherine stepped out of the elevator, trying to place him. He'd said on the phone that they met at a party, but she hadn't been to a party in months. "Mercer Kerrigan," he said, standing just a few paces away from her. It still felt awkward not to shake hands, but no one did that anymore. She smiled, held his gaze, and repeated her own name.

Mercer beckoned her to follow him into the columned space of polished stone. Ten-foot windows let in masonry light from Fifth Avenue. A black conference table lay to Catherine's left. To her right, neon tubes hung on the wall. Shaped into cursive letters spelling PURSUIT, they let out anxious hissing sounds, like the bug zapper at her childhood pool. "Nice place," she said.

"It's okay," he said. "These were a bad choice." He flicked a switch on the wall and the PURSUIT tubes went dead. "My desk is in the back." He led her around a covered billiards table and a folding screen to an area furnished with a desk, a coat stand, a facing aluminum-frame chair, and a dimpled leather daybed. Catherine noticed a pillow, blanket, and canvas satchel stashed neatly below.

He caught her staring. "I don't sleep here if I can help it," he said.

She nodded and thought: *Attractive*. Hawkish and severe in the face, his chin a little prominent, but good skin, nice height, and they weren't far off in age. His deep-set teal eyes were like gaudy buttons sewn in their sockets.

She swallowed against an itchy throat. This wasn't a first date, she reminded herself—it was an interview; *an opportunity you might be interested in* was what he'd told her yesterday afternoon on the phone. And if it meant a paycheck and health insurance she certainly would be. She'd been without both since February.

"Outside—that guy is with you?" she asked. Down on Fifth, a man with white-blond hair cut close to his scalp, a soccer jersey, and a knife-blade neck tattoo. Midthirties. Smiling at her, leaning against an Audi sedan, flicking his cigarette ash in her direction. "Fook, you're lovely," he'd said, in an accent so thick she didn't understand him at first. He nodded at the building's entry. "Go on. Fifth floor."

"Laird," Mercer explained. "Did he say something? I'm sort of still working on his presentation."

"Told me I was lovely," Catherine said. "Is he Scottish?" Scotland was a mess, the second-worst place on Earth, some website had reported the other day, just ahead of India, which was still cleaning up its two-year dead.

"Clients love him, you can imagine. A real-life Glasgow thug. Have a seat."

She did, taking off her coat, draping it on the open chair. "I don't actually know who your clients are," she said. "It's Pursuit? As in of happiness?"

He smiled like she'd just hit him with a witticism. But she was coming clean; she didn't know much about his company beyond the name. How could she? The website was a white screen with a phone number; when you called it, there was a beep and silence.

"I brought my résumé," she said, wondering if she'd been too flip. Mercer's expression and that wry, measuring smile were difficult to read. She'd printed her résumé on heavy linen-stock paper as if to hide how little was on it: the Tramway Foundation job her mother had gotten her, her BA from Vassar, "proficiency in French."

He placed one hand on top of the other on his desk. "I was sorry to hear about the accident. That was in December?"

April's death had made a few headlines, so people knew. "Thanks," Catherine said. "It was a shock."

"I can imagine."

Catherine never knew how to talk about her mother. "Accidental mother," she sometimes said, with just enough crisp emphasis to signal that this was the truth. She grasped for a question to ask. "When did you say we met?"

"Sophie Fulk's place." He laughed at her blank expression. "You don't remember. You were with Krupa and Lorraine and that gang."

At least a year ago. More. But she could have been drunk or high. She didn't remember him.

"How's she doing anyway? Krupa. Expanding her empire?"

"We're sort of out of touch."

"Why's that?"

Catherine smiled uncertainly. Getting dropped by Krupa was another subject she didn't know how to talk about.

"Prize bitch. I wonder why you hung out with her."

"I liked Krupa." She had. Krupa Chatwal, a slim Indian girl who'd gone to Andover with Phillip, who clutched Catherine's hand when they first met as if they'd known each other for years, and exclaimed that she was "by far" the prettiest girl Phillip had ever dated. Later, after two lines of Krupa's coke in the bathroom stall of a West Village speakeasy (a place you had to know six different people to get into), Krupa had pointed at the embossed name on the toilet tank and then at Catherine. Because she *knew*. Phillip must have told her, and Catherine remembered feeling approved of—and then ashamed, and just as quickly craving another line to wipe all her feelings away. Catherine had thousands of dollars of credit card debt and could barely afford the rent on her tiny Bleecker Street walk-up. "I love how *real* you are," Krupa had said later that night as if she knew these things too, her face so close to Catherine's that Catherine thought she might kiss her.

Krupa was a socialite, friends with models and DJs and gentlemanly rich kids like Phillip, but she had a job too, editing *Muck*, this art-and-fashion broadsheet run out of a storefront on Elizabeth Street, and she booked bands for a Lower East Side club, 62—bands who played loud enough to make your stomach turn over. She adored Phillip, who, unlike Catherine, barely drank and never touched drugs and plugged his ears at the shows at 62. Krupa took to calling Catherine, with a kind of punkish approval, "Phillip's toilet princess," and flew the two of them around in the Chatwals' Gulfstream, to Paris for the weekend, to a wedding in Croatia, to a villa in Positano. This was all before the curfews and quarantines—before TX. In the first month of the outbreak, Krupa dragged Catherine and Phillip to restaurants, to house parties, to the Hamptons, to whatever was still open. Krupa swore everyone was overreacting, that you couldn't take something called Texas Flu seriously. Catherine's mother said that too. This would be over in weeks. The key was to keep your head.

Prize bitch. Catherine couldn't think of her that way, couldn't dismiss the fun she'd had—running up her credit card balance, sweeping into parties at Fashion Week, topless sunbathing on the terrace in Positano. Catherine remembered one lovely pink-streaked dawn in New York, on the 62 rooftop, maybe six months before the outbreak. Whatever band was getting interviewed and a photographer shot Krupa and the singer against the railing. Krupa had pointed at Catherine and the photographer had turned and shot her too, a tumbler of Patrón in Catherine's hand, her bare feet in Phillip's lap. In that deliriously happy moment, she saw herself in the frame—the chestnut hair she'd inherited from her mother dropping past her shoulders, her long bare legs, her face in profile, laughing at what somebody had said.

"I know why she hung out with me," Catherine said to Mercer.

"Your mom."

"More the guy I was seeing. But then he died."

"In the thing."

She tried to nod with the appropriate gravity, but Philip's death had never haunted her the way it should have. They'd only dated for nine months and she hadn't told him much about herself. He'd had this patrician, long-wave voice she sometimes had trouble hearing. The sex they'd had had been polite and infrequent. She'd wondered if he was gay.

And *so* many people had died. Three hundred million, fifteen million in the US, roughly 4 percent of the population gone. An almost incomprehensible slaughter. Texas Flu was a nasty, virulent killer—it incubated for a week, becoming increasingly contagious until the viral load spiked: fever, fluid hemorrhaging into the lungs, a fatality rate of about 50 percent. It was novel too, a sort of genetic medley of influenza and Lassa, with the ability to persist in the blood like HIV, the product of what scientists called a rare recombination event. They didn't know when, or exactly how, except the janitor at a Galveston middle school went into work sick after a weeklong vacation to Mexico and gave what he had to a few dozen students. TX—as it came to be known—moved quickly; a cough or sneeze passed it along. Within a week kids were hospitalized, their parents too, then cases all across the country. TX had started its nine-month sprint around the globe. Governments filled hospitals, threw up makeshift cordons in cities. Some countries tried to seal themselves off, militarizing their borders—creating even more panic. In the US the CDC ordered airports to remain open until the very end, built quarantine camps for symptomatic Americans, and transported the dead to enormous burial grounds, places cordoned as biohazards. Everyone knew someone who'd died. The names ran in lists, on the Web, on the news; Catherine remembered Krupa calling in hysterics when she'd seen Phillip's and his parents'. Catherine had closed her laptop—she'd been scanning the names too and listening to the sirens on the street. Krupa's breath had hitched and quavered. "Are you still there?" Catherine had managed a yes and hung up the phone.

She remembered the fear rushing up and out of her. Crying hysterically into her empty fridge—but not, she knew then, for Philip. Because she'd been hungry and scared. Because she'd watched her neighbors, half-covered in plastic, carried out her building's front door and into refrigerated trucks. Because she could smell a sweet rot rising up through her floor. Because she wanted to live.

Finally TX seemed to burn itself out. The US declared the pandemic over, and haltingly—month by month—life began a stunned march back to normal. Curfews were lifted, travel restrictions were eased, public spaces and restaurants quietly reopened. Stock markets rebounded more quickly than anyone thought possible. Catherine had met up with Krupa and the other girls in her circle. A few somber dinner parties. Eventually some nights out. Maybe that was when she'd met Mercer? In any case, she didn't remember.

"Can I ask what we're talking about?" she asked him now. Mercer leaned back, hands behind his neck. He seemed to be turning something over in his mind. "You mentioned a job?"

"Ever feel a generalized sort of annoyance at the world?" he asked her.

She tried to appear pensive, not sure what he meant.

"To give you an example," Mercer said, tapping a steel pen on the wood surface of his desk, then setting it flat with a click. "This other morning on the train a woman is peeling an egg. Holding it in one hand and peeling it with the other, the shell dropping into this Tupperware bowl between her thighs. She eats it like she's in a contest: bam bam bam. Then she's chewing and chewing and chewing, and I'm like: *You hopeless fucking wreck of a human being.* I can't help it. I'm about three rows away, staring through my hand, catching the smell, seeing the yolk on her lips, the, like, membrane and shell on her fingernails. It took everything I had not to stand up, walk over, and sock her in the face."

The tone of Mercer's voice had changed, picking up speed and volume. Catherine shifted in her seat. "Maybe you hadn't had your coffee yet."

"I was questioning her worth as a human being," Mercer finished. "You do that too, I'm sure."

"No."

"Of course you do."

Catherine swallowed against what felt like a sore throat. *Most people simply aren't worth your time,* her mother had said over and over when Catherine was growing up. A pronouncement that had thrilled her with its declarative force—despite the fact that she knew all too well how April Mayville could lump her in with *most people.* She would casually disparage simple things her daughter liked—game shows, French fries, high-top sneakers—and then hit her with this chilly air of disregard. Catherine used to try mimicking it in the mirror: the infinitesimal tilt of the head, the merry sigh, the checking of the watch.

"But you didn't," she said to Mercer.

"I didn't what?"

"Sock the woman in the face."

Mercer trained his gaze on her. "I remember that boyfriend of yours. Sort of curly hair? Nice, but soft. A real slush puppy."

She let that sit for a polite moment and then asked: "Could we talk about the job?" A wave of weariness passed over Mercer's face. He stifled a yawn and gave his cheeks a brisk slap. "Pursuit's basically access," he said. "We tell members where to go: parties, restaurants, clubs. We get them on lists; we get the next bag for their girlfriends. Also exotic stuff: A week at one of those islands where no one ever got sick. One member wanted an Italian sailboat outfitted with radar equipment and weapons. That took four weeks to sort out. Another wanted to shoot a snow leopard in the wild. Where can you do such a thing with the full blessing of the local authorities? Kyrgyzstan. Rich men will pay this, like, staggering monthly fee for a fixer working a headset and terminal in midtown. A lot of men will. With zero advertising or publicity, Pursuit's a runaway train. But now I'm onto something different. Same principle: men want relief. They're tired of feeling hunkered down and worried about the future. Which is only getting scarier. With these, what, propagators? You've read about these guys?"

Catherine nodded. People who went around coughing and spitting in public. Kids mostly, anarchists. Nobody knew what their agenda was, or if they actually had TX. The Department of Health called them bioterrorists.

"They only bring out the government's Big Brother side. Those MED sensors? People think it's just subway turnstiles, mailboxes, but they're actually *everywhere*. Two, three per block. We're blips on a DOH screen, just sitting here. Are you okay?"

Catherine's eyes were watering; she felt a cough coming on, just as it had in the screening center the other day. You couldn't cough in a job interview, sitting six feet away from your prospective boss. "Do you have any—any water?"

"Sure." Mercer stood up, opened a panel in the wall, took a bottle out of a recessed fridge, and handed it over.

"My dad cut his MED card up," she said, taking a big swig. "Dropping off the biosurveillance map, he called it."

Mercer spread his hands as if that proved his point. "Men want a break from feeling fatalistic about the state of the world."

"Dad's a little paranoid," she said. The water had helped, but the tickle was back; she lightly cleared her throat. "Sorry—I just have something in the back of my—"

"It's more hands-on than what I've been doing with Pursuit. Which poses a problem. My debutantes in midtown don't impress in person. I need someone with poise. Some honest-to-god pedigree."

Catherine almost laughed. He was flattering her—a girl with a three-figure checking balance, a coffee-spotted blouse, a cut on her stomach from climbing out a screening center window. Still, she liked it. She could listen to it all day.

"I'm not quite ready to launch, so I'll start you in the call center. Pay's not great, but I do benefits, and when the new project takes off you'll have an equity stake. If you want the job."

Just like that. Startled, Catherine tried to thank him, to ask how soon she could start, to ask what she would actually be doing, but a cough fluttered out of her chest before she could. She threw an arm over her lips to stifle it.

2

"Who's she?"

A teenage girl stood beside the Scottish guy, both leaning against the front of the building, standing in a wash of springtime sun. "Oi," he said to her. "*Oi*. It's Cathy, yeah?"

Catherine glanced at them—the girl had short, slightly greasy brown hair, darker than her own, and it curled under her ears. She wore faded jeans and a too-tight crewneck sweater. Catherine pulled her jacket around her and took in deep lungfuls of the chilly morning air. It was going to be okay. *It was going to be okay.* Catherine repeated this three times over, as if casting a spell. She'd call the number on the business card Mercer had given her, explain why she'd practically jogged out of his office. She was fine, obviously, just something had caught in her throat and she hadn't wanted to go on coughing in front of him. How soon could she start?

Was she okay? It was Tuesday, which meant she'd had a sore itch around her tonsils for five days, and now there was this cough plus what felt like a thin ribbon of pressure between her eyes. Her screening deadline was a week from Friday but if you felt anything like a fever or a cough, you weren't supposed to wait. The virus hadn't burned out after all. It had simply become harder to detect until a host presented symptoms. There were antivirals now, but they only worked if you took them the minute you felt sick. The drugs were supposed to be carefully rationed—but if you had a good private

doctor and money to spend, you could get as much as you wanted.
Same thing with the TX rapid test. If you had a private doctor it took
all of fifteen minutes. Catherine used to be in and out of Dr. Cohen's
on her lunch break. But no private doctors in New York would test
an uninsured person like Catherine. That's what the public health
centers were for, but the lines were brutal and you heard about false
positives, about people carted off to quarantine for no reason—and
after panicking and climbing out the bathroom window on Spring
Street yesterday, she couldn't go back. Maybe she wouldn't have to.
If she started at Pursuit tomorrow, enrolled in the health plan, she
could see Dr. Cohen that evening, or Thursday morning at the latest. Two days from now—she pictured it: waltzing in, getting her
swab, her results. There hadn't been a confirmed case of TX in the
Northeast for almost a year, so she probably had a cold—people still
caught colds. Or just hay fever. Or maybe she had nothing at all.

Ignoring the Scottish man and the girl, she fell into step behind a dog walker tugged along by a parade of dachshunds. It was
past ten in the morning and the Fifth Avenue traffic was light, the
sidewalks starting to empty out. Budding trees in concrete plant-
ers threw mixed shadows onto the pavement. Catherine passed a
hat and T-shirt vendor, a newsagent, and then a bus shelter with a
bright red poster behind glass: FEEL SOMETHING, DO SOMETHING
and the Department of Health shield at the bottom. She put her
hand to her forehead. Cool, dry. No fever. One of the orderlies at the
screening center yesterday had confirmed as much by gunning her
with his temperature scanner and moving placidly down the line.

Catherine told herself she was just run down. She hadn't been
sleeping well; she'd been dreaming of her mother's car turning on
the slippery highway, a tree rising up to meet it. She dreamed of
April blinking at the EMTs out of her crumpled cockpit, her eyes
like lights at the bottom of a sinkhole.

The dreams were new, and reassuring in a way. Back in December, when the phone had rung—four a.m., her father's tight voice, "this is going to be hard to hear, duck"—she decided the warm-water calm that filled her was shock and that it was perfectly natural to want more than anything, at the news of your mother's death, to go back to sleep.

It *was* shock. In the days leading up to the funeral, she kept going over, in this relentless, robotic way, the last conversation she'd had with April. Her mother had called her from Richmond, and Catherine had been too tired and depressed to conjure small talk. She'd simply answered her mother's questions truthfully: the Tramway job was dull—rote secretarial work—and no, Richard Tramway hadn't invited her to any benefits for the spring, and there was zero news on the boyfriend front. She might have been flattered by her mother's interest—April generally preferred to let information come to her. But she mostly wanted the conversation to end.

"So you're depressed."

"Am I?"

"You could get pregnant."

"With who?"

"Whom. Any nice boy."

"Is that a serious suggestion?"

Catherine heard April take a sip of something—the Chablis she drank too much of. "Say what you will about babies, but they keep you *busy*."

A novel feeling ambushed Catherine: pity. Her mother had been aimless since the Mayville board had forced her to sell her stake almost a decade before. Buying, furnishing, and selling a series of apartments in New York; sitting on charity boards; and carrying on affairs with a half-dozen men. What did it all amount to? Why had she called? But Catherine didn't believe it was her job to tease out the answers. "I'm plenty busy," Catherine had said. "Busy isn't the problem."

"Well, fine. Take it under advisement." Another sip. "I love you, sweetheart."

That was strange too. Declarations of love were not her mother's style.

The fundamental thing between them was that April had never wanted children and had left parenting duties to nannies and babysitters. It was how she'd been raised. April's mother had died of cancer when she was five and her father, Lionel Mayville, had packed her off to boarding school the minute he could. Then he'd dropped dead of a massive coronary April's senior year at Vassar, leaving her a controlling stake in Mayville Toilets & Sinks, the third largest manufacturer of bathroom fixtures in the country. Following the advice of her lawyer, April gave herself a dummy title and a salary in the low millions. She had no idea what her responsibilities should be, but that didn't keep her from requesting marketing plans, spreadsheets, and sales reports as if she did. The board ignored April for as long as they could, even as they paid her extravagant travel expenses and let her sit in on their meetings. Catherine's earliest memories were of watching her mother set her Vuitton suitcases by the front door and impatiently check her watch, waiting for the cab to the airport. She had Mayville company business in Paris, in São Paulo, in London, she said—though she probably didn't. She just didn't want to be home.

Take me with you, Catherine had thought more times than she could count.

In high school, Catherine would find her mother in the library peering at Mayville documents over a glass of champagne. "That figure there is the one that has to get bigger," she would say. "If it doesn't you call Julian and tell him to fire someone." Catherine had figured out that this was just talk. Her mother had no real role at the company. And it would be only a matter of months before Julian Sebold—the Mayville CEO—allied himself with several minority shareholders and threatened to sue. In retaliation April hired her own legal team and sold her stake to a Swiss conglomerate, who quickly took control of the company and closed two of the Mayville manufacturing plants in southern Virginia.

Local news reports juxtaposed layoffs of glaze engineers and pipe setters with the windfall April Mayville and family would enjoy from the sale. But April's family enjoyed no such windfall—just April, who bought a fractional share of a twelve-seat Sikorsky helicopter, chartered flights to Gstaad and to a Patagonia ranch house, and committed millions to charitable organizations to stay on their social calendars. In the end, she handed an astonishing amount to a boyfriend named Marcel, a Lebanese real estate tycoon, to fund a luxury tower in Beirut. "April, I'm afraid, made a few unfortunate investments," Geoff Jenkins, the soft-spoken family lawyer, told Catherine and her father when they'd gathered in his wood-paneled conference room in Richmond to read the will two days before the funeral. Catherine had long suspected her mother's fortune couldn't survive her spending of it; she'd also steeled herself against the prospect of being cut out entirely. And yet when Jenkins confirmed how little would be left after the various debts were paid—"thirty-odd, ah, *thousand* dollars"—Catherine felt the wind go out of her.

At the funeral, she sat beside her father in that cold, crowded church and listened to the minister go on and on about how April Mayville had inspired people with her graciousness and style. "April had *a flair for living*," the minister said. "A generosity of spirit."

Catherine wanted to stand up and tell the congregation that she'd never been particularly generous to *her*. She wanted to tell them about the way April used to wonder aloud if Catherine was gaining weight beneath her slouchy pants and sweaters, or why she wouldn't wear makeup or even the littlest heel, or why she hadn't been asked to join the social committee at St. Ann's, a tiny Richmond girls' school where the cafeteria had linen napkins and everyone wore white dresses at graduation.

Catherine felt her face go hot and her eyes fill with tears as the minister ended her remembrance. They all stood up to sing a hymn and Catherine thought, *Get back to New York.* With the kids who never wore masks on the subway, who coughed with their mouths open, who wiped their noses with their hands. You wanted to *smack* those kids. Her father thought she was crazy to stay in such a crowded place. But Catherine was desperate to get back. She turned to look at him and instead saw her mother right beside her in the pew, her ghost face headlight bright, her long eyelashes fluttering, her emerald-studded ring like a medieval weapon. *You're your mother's daughter,* she said in a hushed whisper. *A Mayville to the ground. Mayvilles don't get sick.*

April really had believed that. She'd never worn a mask. She claimed she didn't know anyone who'd died, which wasn't true. Her neighbors were gone by the end of the first pandemic month. April simply refused to acknowledge their deaths.

New York was where one was *supposed* to be, she'd always said. So Catherine had skipped the reception she'd done all the planning for (because her father wouldn't or couldn't marshal the energy), had driven straight to the airport and taken the first standby flight that would have her.

3

"Not to worry," Mercer said on the phone. "I figured it was something like that."

Catherine propped her forearms on the cool kitchen countertop, phone at her ear, amazed at how smoothly he'd accepted her excuse: a bit of breakfast granola down the wrong pipe. "That's great, Mercer. Thank you—thanks for understanding. People are so paranoid about anything that looks like a . . ." *Symptom,* but she wouldn't say it. "Anyway, thank you."

"Start Monday?" Catherine couldn't be sure, but she thought she heard a girl's laughter in the background. "And that other project I mentioned? Don't say a word about it to Samantha. As far as she knows you're just there to work the phones." He then apologized for the pay. "And Samantha's a slave driver, but just keep telling yourself the post is temporary. You're learning the ropes while I ready this new thing."

She said it all sounded fine—but it wasn't really. Monday was six days away. She heard the girl's voice in the background again. "Dude, get off the *phone.*"

"Good," Mercer said. "We'll have fun. I promise."

Catherine said good-bye and ended the call, set the phone down, and pushed it across the countertop.

Monday. Monday would be okay. *We'll have fun.* Focus on that. Because she hadn't had anything that looked like fun since Krupa

stopped calling, since she'd lost her mother, since Richard Tramway had let her go with a four-week severance in February (he
didn't really need her, had only taken her on as a favor to April;
"Keep in touch," he'd said). There was Maggie, an old Vassar friend,
a curvy blonde who was always game for a drink, but nights out
with Maggie typically ended after the girl's third vodka soda when
she started scanning the bar for any available man of comparable
age to go home with. Maggie's desperation embarrassed Catherine. She couldn't hide it. "Know what your problem is?" Maggie had
boozily shouted into Catherine's ear the last time they'd gone out
together. "You think you're too good for this." *This* was a crowded,
dank-smelling basement bar on Ludlow Street—and a couple of
years before she'd been in Positano toasting the sunset. Catherine
felt exposed at the time. "Maybe I am," she shouted back—a bit
drunk herself—set her drink on the pitted wood bar, and left. A
revved-up motor of superiority drove her all the way home, up the
stairs, and into the bedroom of her next-door neighbor, the investment banker she'd lately been flirting with, whom she'd encountered
on the landing patting his pockets for his keys. She ignored the
smell of beer and cheap cologne that rolled off of him. Two things
she focused on: his finely shaped jaw and the Film Forum ticket stub
on his dresser. There'd been zero kissing, of course—you didn't kiss
people you didn't know—and he'd insisted on fucking her from behind because it was safer. "Plus," he told her afterward, "eye contact
makes me lose my hard-on." What exactly was she too good for, she
wondered, gathering her clothes and jogging across the landing.

It hadn't been a good winter. A mouse darted out from under
Catherine's oversized radiator cover and she toasted it with her glass
of water and drank; the water felt so delicious and cool against her
throat that she felt momentarily brave. She wouldn't let the mouse
get to her, nor her cough, nor the size of her apartment—a narrow
one-bedroom cut from its larger neighbor by a flimsy slab of drywall.

She'd let herself be carried on a drift of optimism. She might even call her dad—she owed him a call. *You're not sick*, he'd say. Her panicked stunt in the screening center bathroom had been rational behavior. Crazy to put yourself in government hands. Only sheep followed DOH rules. The job he'd think less of—so maybe keep that to herself. Just describe the previous morning. Make it seem like an adventure. Her first-ever trip to the center on Spring Street. Coughing in the line, feeling the stares drilling in, heading to the ladies' room.

So she called him, for the first time in weeks. "You climbed out a *window?*" he asked—his voice raspy on the line—when she was done with her story.

"I couldn't go the regular way," she told him. "There were guards."

Actually, she shouldn't have put herself in the Green Zone at all. When she'd joined the back of the line, she'd been confronted by sternly worded signs that read the room was to be kept symptom free. No fever. No cough. She'd told herself that it was only the barest tickle in her throat—and no way was she going to the Orange Zone, clear on the other side of the building. There were actual sick people there—who knew what they had? Safer to be here, Catherine decided, in this enormous, cacophonous space, lit by high-banked fluorescents. She listened to the whooshing from containment vents, the curtains raking back and forth across cubicles at the far end of the room, the nurses in plastic suits shouting, "*Next!*"

But then, after a half hour in line, a run of coughs had climbed up out of her throat. She'd slapped her arm over her mouth, stifling them as quietly as she could. Hostile stares front and back. A space formed around her in line. A guy in a Mets jersey, strapping on a face mask, eyes wide, looked ready to launch at her.

"Catherine, that wasn't smart," her father said. "Going there wasn't smart."

"The DOH has better things to do than track me down."

"I wouldn't be too sure."

"If they want me they can find me." That was true. The hidden Department of Health sensors in subway turnstiles, mailboxes, street lamps—*two, three per block,* Mercer had said—read biometric data stored in your MED card or in those new indestructible bracelets they were making homeless people wear. The sensors relayed this information—your identity and the date of your last TX test—to DOH servers. Scientists couldn't explain the lack of resistance—why you could recover from TX and then get sick again. Nor could they explain the isolated outbreaks that started flaring up and burning out in hopscotch fashion after the pandemic had ended.

The virus was persisting in the population. Hiding in T cells was one hypothesis, undetected by the immune system. A small town in Iowa had been wiped out as recently as three months ago. Before that it was a factory in a Chinese industrial city—thousands killed. Before that a district in Paris, a village in southern Sudan, a swath of downtown Auckland.

Officials said the best line of defense was vigilance. Report symptoms immediately. Yours. Family members'. Friends'. Get the TX test every three months. *Ninety Days . . . It's the Law* ran the ads. Carry your MED card at all times. Don't gamble with symptoms. Don't travel if you're sick. These messages had been drummed into the public through news and magazine stories and stacks of bestselling how-to books on surviving another full-scale TX pandemic—which would come, the scientists said. It was just a matter of time.

Her father believed none of this. TX had *obviously* been engineered. "A recombination event? *Such* bullshit," he said. TX was a weaponized virus, made in a lab. He'd told her so a thousand times. Which was why she kept the phone calls to a minimum. Too much of him was exhausting. Within weeks of the funeral her father was e-mailing her encrypted links to blog posts about the CIA and the CDC, written by conspiracy nuts—personal friends of his—who believed what he did. *Massive cover-up*, he would say. *Why do you think they created the DOH?* Actually it was hard to know exactly what he believed, or if something was truly wrong with him. Some days he seemed like a caring father who missed his daughter, who worried about her living in New York, who was maybe a little too much in his own head. At other times he seemed like a genuinely crazy person who believed government agents were tapping his phone. The last time she'd seen him, a month after the funeral, he'd been a wreck. "There's no limit to what they're capable of," he told her. The house was a disaster—heaps of old newspapers everywhere, piles of smelly laundry in the hallways, two Canada Dry bottles half-full of urine on the floor beside his favorite chair. She stayed up most of the first night cleaning, a marathon session of Windex and paper towels and bleach that her father had said over and over again wasn't necessary. But then the next morning Catherine caught him shuffling wide-eyed from the gleaming dining room table to a wiped-clean window to a dusted lampshade, as if on a museum tour.

Her dad's voice in the phone grew insistent: "You should come visit."

"Can't."

"Why? There's no job keeping you there."

"As a matter of fact," she started—but then held off.

"What?"

"Nothing. I've got a lead."

He grunted skeptically. "How are you for money?"

"Fine," she said. Not true. She had eight hundred dollars in her checking account, her Visa debt was above nine thousand—and her mother's estate would not be coming to the rescue. It was still in probate and Catherine's share only amounted to about eleven grand after taxes. It would pay out months from now.

"I can send you a little if you need it," Jack said.

She'd regret it later if she let him. "Dad, honestly, I'm fine."

Nothing for moments, then: "New York's dangerous, duck. With that cough? A health cop could pick you up off the street."

She interrupted him: "I was in a good mood when I called."

"Come home and we'll take care of you."

"We who? You and your weirdo friends?"

Her father let out a frustrated sigh. "You know I can't say—"

"On an open line," she said, interrupting him and letting out a sigh of her own.

4

Was he crazy? It was a hard question to answer. Her father had always had an antiestablishment streak, back to his days as an anti-Reagan, no-nukes firebrand at Brown. Like her mother, he was from an old Richmond family, but the Duvals had run through their money a generation before Jack was born. So after a freewheeling period in his twenties traveling through Nicaragua and Venezuela, Jack had had to shave his beard, cut his hair, shelve his Minutemen records and Chomsky books, and find work selling insurance, then classified ads, then, finally, pharmaceuticals. The Pfizer job had been steady for six years—but when he complained to his immediate boss about the fraudulent sales pitch on a powerful new antipsychotic, and then complained to the regional managers above him, he was fired. That led to a long legal battle and a $2.3 billion criminal fine Pfizer paid to the US government—the largest such fine in history. Jack Duval, briefly, became famous, a drug rep who knew Pfizer was breaking the law and decided to do something about it. Pfizer paid him $15 million and pulled the drug from the market, and Jack never worked a full-time job again, devoting himself, instead, to restoring vintage MGs and slowly but surely giving all of his settlement money to his favorite NGOs and political groups.

To Catherine he was a stay-at-home dad with shaggy hair and a paunch, as reliable at getting food on the table and driving carpool as he was eccentric. Early on, his tirades over the papers, the way he'd stomp around, or send the front page sailing across the room, or read from it aloud in a mockingly authoritarian baritone—so often the business section, stories about windfall profits or CEOs and their emperors' salaries—had made her laugh. Every performance ended with him making fun of himself: "Quack, quack, quack," he'd say, flapping his arms, shaking his head at his own agitation. (Inspiring, following a logic Catherine could no longer recall, *him* giving *her* the nickname "duck.") She used to like how weird and theatrical he could be. And she loved the way his beard would grow in day after day, run through with scraggly gray, until he finally shaved it all off and his cheeks felt miraculously soft to the touch.

Best of all were Saturdays in fall and winter, when he took her to the country club squash courts. She'd listen to the squeak of sneakers and the slap of the ball and watch him snap his racket and gracefully spring back to the painted T. She'd watch until she got hungry and then go sit near the refreshment table, where one of the sweaty players would offer her a sports bar or half a banana if she smiled in just the right imploring way. Once, standing on her tiptoes, she'd fished a brightly wrapped bar out of the straw basket, and a hand had clamped down on her shoulder—a man in damp wristbands and white shorts, veins knotty under the pale blue skin of his calf. He'd appeared out of nowhere. "Not for you, young lady." She dropped the contraband, but the man held her still, looking at her closely. "Where's that father of yours?" She'd squirmed free and bolted, checking all four of the courts, and finally found him in the men's locker room—a place she'd gotten too old for. She passed pale, hairy legs, heaps of yellowing towels, gigantic bellies, a saggy naked man with ash-gray pubic hair. There was a great commotion at her appearance; she buried her face in her dad's shower-wet knees, begging to be taken home.

"What's the lesson, duck?" Jack had asked in the car.

Only seven years old, but Catherine ventured an answer: "Don't take? Ask?"

"The lesson is: rich people are monsters."

"Aren't we rich?" she'd asked.

"Your mother is."

She remembered this line, not because it was any big revelation—by seven she'd figured out that her parents were on opposing sides of some endless grudge match—but because it was the first time she heard a funny note in her dad's voice, something that bothered her but that she didn't have a word for.

Hypocrite. If rich people were monsters—why be a member of that country club? And why marry April Mayville? They'd met a few months after the news of the Pfizer fine and April thought this Jack Duval was foolish for taking such a big swing at his employer. "You should have been grateful," she teased him. "Giving a scruffy boy like you a paycheck." He was handsome though—long and lean and dressed in corduroy shorts and huaraches, while all the other young men at the club wore loafers, pleated shorts, and peach-colored polos. She asked him what exactly he'd blown the whistle on and he tried to explain—but lost her quickly. "Poor Pfizer," she teased him.

"Want to know how much two point three billion dollars is?" he responded seriously. "Two weeks of their sales."

As if he wasn't proud of what he'd done. As if he didn't consider himself a Robin Hood hero, a David taking down a corporate Goliath. He'd loved the media attention, his appearances on the *Today* show, on *Oprah*, speaking to the *New York Times*, the *Wall Street Journal*—to whomever called him.

This was all before Catherine was born, but she'd heard both of them talk about it—him with weary longing. "Back then people actually *cared* about things," he said.

Why not divorce April when it was clear she was cheating on him? The older Catherine got the more the irony bothered her: Here was a man who'd stood up to a giant corporation, who railed at news anchors every day at six p.m., but couldn't even raise his voice at his wife when she disappeared on trips, when she wore mysterious gifts around the house—jewels, dresses, watches. Or when she would sit in the back garden to take private calls on her cell phone from Marcel, saying loud enough to be heard: "Of course, darling, missing you *terribly*."

They *had* been in love. Their honeymoon had been six weeks—France, Egypt, China—a money-no-object trip that "could have gone on and on and on," April liked to say. There were framed pictures around the house—the two of them in the bow of a felucca on the Nile in Aswan, looking thin and serious and sun-kissed—but despite this evidence Catherine couldn't imagine them happy. April had come back pregnant, which wasn't her plan at all, and Jack hated the parties she took him to. He wanted April at home, with him, but April couldn't stand being cooped up in the big house she'd inherited from her father and didn't have the patience for Jack's political fervor. "Sometimes I think he's simply cuckoo," she told Catherine.

Sometimes Catherine did too. Especially now that he spent most of his days taking rounds on the inner loop of his own head, or meeting at coffee shops with friends to trade conspiracy theories. Over the phone he'd carry on about Galveston as if resuming an interrupted conversation with someone else. He'd say something about a lab knocked sideways by Hurricane Martha and that you were a sucker if you believed the official story.

There's no limit to any of it, he kept saying. *The lies and deceptions.* The first time she'd heard this refrain had been two years ago, on a visit to Richmond after TX had been declared contained and the travel ban had been lifted. Catherine felt both stunned by and giddy from what she'd been through: stocking her kitchen with food, plowing through that, then the rations left at her door by the National Guard, then going hungry, listening to the rioting and gunfire carry over from Washington Square Park. "So, Dad, we survived!" she said, freshly arrived from the Richmond train station, fixing her first gin and tonic in a dusty glass, noticing the dust on everything, the state of the house, but feeling cautiously celebratory anyway.

"Survived what?" her dad had said from his favorite armchair, his laptop open on his thighs, his smudged reading glasses reflecting the display. "The biggest criminal fraud in our nation's history?"

It snowed that afternoon, a crystalline carpet of snow settling on the walk and turning parked cars into gentle swells of white. She'd be stranded by the storm for four days—two more than she'd intended to stay—and would spend much of the time gloomily staring out the window thinking how sparkling and untouched and new everything looked, how irrevocably the world had changed, while inside here was a stubbornly familiar problem: father and daughter, proximate but not remotely close.

Why on earth had she come? Her mother lay, as promised, on a sun-drenched beach two thousand miles to the south. "Oh, don't visit for my sake, darling," April had said when Catherine called. "I won't even *be* here. The minute they open the airport, I'm on the first flight to . . . wherever. Barbados."

Jack showed little interest in anything besides his laptop and beloved armchair. Eating and sleeping no longer seemed part of his routine. Magically he seemed to get all the nourishment he now needed out of the house's wireless connection.

"The guy they've got running this new department—you know his background?" he asked. "Medicine? An MD? No, of course not. Not to run a *health* agency." Was that food on his shirt? An orange-brown crust above the breast pocket. It looked like peanut butter. So he *had* eaten. "Intelligence, duck. You tell me why they need a spook running something called the Department of Health."

Most of the time his questions were rhetorical. She never knew when he wanted an answer.

"Because there's no limit to it," he said. "The deception. The arrogance."

Catherine left him then, in the library, curiously his favorite room in the house, damp and cold thanks to the marble floors and the casement windows, and musty from the old books and the wet bar tucked behind hinged cabinet doors.

She went to the kitchen to make herself a pot of coffee. "Duck, come back." That was him in the dining room. "Want you to see something."

She delayed. She unfolded the top of the coffee bag, took a deep sniff of the beans, ran the water into the coffeemaker, rinsed out the pot, ground the beans, flipped the switch, and watched the coffee go drip, drip, drip.

"The school's right here," he said when she came back to the library. He was bent over the long mahogany table, utterly absorbed in a large, unfolded road map of southern Texas. He snapped the map with his finger.

Ground zero, people called it. Reporters had doggedly reconstructed the same events: Jose Alvarez, the school's janitor, wakes up Monday morning after his trip to his parents' farm in Mexico coughing, feverish, but the school is already short staffed. *Can't miss another day*, he thinks; Hurricane Martha has put his wife and two brothers out of work. So in he goes.

Her dad yanked a pen out of his breast pocket and inked one X and then another less than a mile away, on a wider section of the island. "The CDC has a lab here." He connected the two Xs with a heavy black line. "Or they had one. You can get satellite images online. Today it's just turned earth."

Peanut butter on his shirt. Confirmed. She was close enough to be sure. Close enough also to smell him, that brown-sugar odor she liked, plus an old, airless funk, like the inside of an old shoe, that she didn't.

"Hurricane Martha took the lab out and released god knows what they were working on. Alvarez didn't catch it in Mexico."

She sipped her coffee and warmed her hands on the mug. "Pretty wild stuff, Dad."

He wore a startlingly clear and focused expression: hostility and hurt. He'd gotten this map out for her benefit. "You think it's too much?" he asked. "You think it's far-fetched that our own government—"

"I'm gonna watch some TV."

"There's no limit, Catherine."

"To the deception," she said, walking away from him. "The . . . whatever, bad behavior. I hear you."

5

A text signal from her phone startled Catherine awake. Whipping away the blanket, she sat upright, disoriented, a hair implant infomercial on the TV. She found the remote's off button. The dead screen was a decent enough mirror; she looked a little hounded, a little panicked. The clock on the cable box told her it was past two in the morning—she'd only been asleep for a couple of hours.

The text was from Mercer. *Need you to get screened before you start. See Sandy Robeson, best doc in the city. Here's address.*

Catherine responded immediately: *Yes, of course. Will do.* And then coughed violently into her hands. She tried to stifle the next run, hoping her neighbors couldn't hear. She stood up out of bed. Her throat felt ragged and raw and no matter how much water she drank, the cough wouldn't go away. She went to the bathroom, opened her mouth wide, and inspected the pillowy inflammation. She was fine, she thought, making herself tea with honey. She *had* to be. She found some Maker's Mark in the back of the cabinet and poured that in as well.

Another text: *Robeson can see you at 9. He'll have forms for you to sign. Ok?*

She texted back: *Sure. Thank you.*

The bourbon soothed her throat and let her sleep for a few hours. In the morning, she called the number Mercer had sent her and the

receptionist seemed to know who she was and confirmed her appointment. Catherine strapped on a mask and caught a crowded 8
bus to Third Avenue. From there she hurried up to Eighteenth and
by nine she was standing beside a heap of uncollected garbage bags,
in front of an elegant limestone town house. She climbed the steps,
her hand on the cast-iron railing to a paneled door. She searched the
entry call buttons, pushed the one labeled ROBESON, ACETOR CLINIC,
and an embedded camera swiveled in its glass globe. The door
clicked. Inside, she passed beneath a noisy vent to a steel staircase.
On the second floor, a door marked ACETOR opened to a luminously
white waiting room. A young woman behind a desk nodded when
Catherine said her name and that Mercer Kerrigan had arranged
for her to see Dr. Robeson.

"Have a seat," the receptionist said before disappearing down
a hall. Catherine took one of the leather chairs near the street-side
windows. The walls had a freshly painted smell, and the receptionist's station was immaculate: no medical files, no coffee cups, not
even a phone. There was nothing to read, not a magazine, not even
one of the scary brochures you always found in rooms like these.

The receptionist returned wearing nurse's scrubs and a micro-
fiber mask, and beckoned Catherine to follow her into a treatment
room. This too looked brand-new, with a pristine examination table
and a countertop full of medical supplies: gloves, swabs, bandages.
The woman put gloves on, peeled the plastic sheathing off a swab,
and told Catherine to rock her head backward. With a quick, practiced motion she inserted the swab deep into Catherine's nostril,
gave it a twirl, and dropped it into a vial. She then exited the room
without a word.

Catherine blotted her tearing eyes with the back of her hand—
no matter how gently that was done, it always made her eyes water.
Sitting on the examination table, she checked her watch. She'd have
her answer in minutes. After five, Catherine slid off the table and

started pacing the room. After ten, she felt panic welling up. She cracked open the examination room door and looked both ways down the empty hall, wondering what was going on. She forced herself back to the exam table and told herself to *relax*, to close her eyes—nothing she could do but wait.

Finally, a doctor in his midforties came in carrying a folder. He was fit and handsome, his skin richly tan against his white physician's jacket and face mask. He spoke loudly and clearly so she would understand him through the microfiber: "Sign these and we can start the procedure." He opened the folder and three forms fell into her lap.

"Procedure?" Catherine asked.

"The NDA you should read closely. The legal penalties are severe if you disclose anything about Cyto. Important that you understand that." There was stubble on his neck and he wore a wedding ring beneath his latex gloves. "It goes in quite easily. Takes five minutes. Just need your signature." He pointed at the forms.

She took the pen he offered her.

"I don't understand," she said, reading the word "Cytofit" in bold at the top of the form.

"Small of your back. Size of a teardrop. No one explained this to you?"

She shook her head. The text on the second form was tiny and blurred, as if it had been photocopied too many times.

"I'm . . ." Her voice quavered now. "Do I have it?"

"Swabs can be inconclusive. Nobody admits that but it's true. You said you had a cough? Sore throat?"

"Yeah." But she hadn't mentioned either. "Am I okay?"

"You're going to be." Just the slightest edge of impatience came into his voice. "If you have it, you won't anymore. Regardless, you'll be immune."

"I thought immunity wasn't possible."

"It wasn't."

She looked again at the forms.

"We're covering all the costs."

"Who?"

"Acetor," he said, as if she should know the word. He crossed his arms against his chest, waiting. "Nice to know the right people, huh?"

She blinked at him, not sure what to say to that. She looked at the words "testing phase" along with a list of possible side effects: fever, nausea, coughing fits.

The nurse came in behind the doctor and set a sterile gown on the counter. "Shouldn't be long," she said brightly, and left.

Robeson was still waiting. Her throat did hurt. She did have a cough. She wanted to believe him. So she signed—signed everything.

Minutes later, dressed in the gown, Catherine was led by the nurse farther down the corridor, deeper into the clinic. She smelled more fresh paint and the tart, synthetic aroma of new carpet. Through a doorway, banks of lights blasted a stainless-steel table in a small operating suite. "Don't be nervous," the nurse said through her mask. Catherine did as she was told, lying stomach-down on the table. She shut her eyes; the nurse opened her gown and draped a lightweight sheet over her. The table was heated somehow, but she shivered as the nurse spread a cold ointment in the region of her lower spine. Within seconds, numbness crept up to the middle of her back. The doctor came in. He said, "Good girl," though Catherine didn't know to whom this was directed. She heard the click of a metal instrument tray. She listened carefully, but what he was doing to her was noiseless in the room's chapel quiet. Painless too. A jar came open with a suction-y pop.

"Congratulations," Robeson said. She sat in her bra and skirt, her legs dangling off the examination table, trying to focus on the cold, reassuring pressure of his fingers near the stitches on her lower back. "You may feel some discomfort in the coming days. Dizziness, a bit of fever. Don't worry. To prime itself, the Cyto releases a small combo dose shortly after insertion. I'd tell you the names of the serums but you wouldn't know them."

"Do I go home?"

Robeson nodded, and reapplied a fresh bandage with tape, peeled off his gloves, and dropped them into a canister on the wall. He looked so pleased with everything, so upbeat. "The Cyto has a tiny reservoir, which we'll refill for you should you ever need it. Because this is still in its testing phase you still need to keep to your screening schedule. And, remember . . ." He put a finger to his lips, and she nodded like a grade-schooler. Robeson patted her shoulder and gestured that she could put her shirt on. "Why so glum? You're a lucky girl."

THE

HIDEAWAY

6

"You should ask me what it's like up there," said Frances, taking another drag on her cigarette.

"What's it like up there?" Catherine flattened her tone so that Frances would understand how little she was interested in conversation. Across the street, a group of tourists herded behind a woman with a folded pink umbrella. Every one of them wore a mask, some standard white, others plaid, paisley, striped, or printed with Chanel or Louis Vuitton logos. Steam curlicued out of a manhole, blocking Catherine's view.

Frances smiled through smoke. "Sucky. A dead vibe. You do nothing but MRs all day long, and Sammy's on your ass if you fall behind."

Catherine turned her face to the morning sun pouring down the narrow corridor of West Thirty-Third Street. In her peripheral vision she saw Frances wave her cigarette in the air. "Hey, I'm trying to warn you."

You're making me late. When Catherine closed her eyes, plasmatic blobs sailed right to left; when they were open, gnats needled through points of light. "Totally normal," Dr. Robeson had told her over the phone. "That's the priming process I told you about. Let it run its course. In twenty-four hours you'll be fine." It had taken a week but here it was Thursday morning, and she was ready to get her mind on other things. Mercer had texted her: *All ok? I'll tell S you are ready to start?* She couldn't imagine what to put into a reply—did he know what she'd just been through? What the last week had been like? She simply texted, *Yes, all ok.* Within ten minutes she received an e-mail from Samantha—*Mercer tells me you're coming in. Day shift starts at 830 shrp* and an address on Thirty-Third Street. *Great. See you then!* Catherine had written back, wishing, after clicking send, that she'd left off the exclamation point.

So what? She was excited for a change of scene. She'd woken up at dawn, killed as much time as she could in the apartment, and then decided to walk all the way there, thinking the exercise would do her good. It was early but the coffee vendors and bagel shops were busy. She checked out the summer dresses brightening the store windows along Fifth Avenue. She walked through Madison Square Park because it was clean and lush and patrolled. She turned onto Thirty-Third Street and felt awake, alert; she felt endorphins blinking on inside her like Christmas lights. There was dizziness maybe, but she definitely felt better than she had in days—so much so that she'd offered a familiar, even sisterly smile to the girl coming down the street from the other direction, the girl she'd seen outside Mercer's office the week before, apparently showing up for work herself. The girl gave Catherine a queen-of-England wave with her cigarette hand and introduced herself as Frances. "You're Catherine," she'd added. "Hang on—let me finish this." Catherine kept her distance. Smokers had died in disproportionate numbers and the consensus was healthy lungs at all costs.

"Samantha hates it that I don't take her shit."

Catherine checked her watch. "I should go up," she said.

"Two more minutes," Frances said. "Come on. Hang out." The words came hard and petulant, on a windy breath. There was something in her voice Catherine recognized—maybe loneliness? Frances flipped her hair out of her face, dragged on the cigarette, and dropped her voice conspiratorially. "So, Mercer told me."

"Told you what?"

"That you were this hot socialite."

Were. Catherine heard the word loud and clear. "I wasn't."

"Liar. I've seen the party pictures. I saw that big piece."

In the *New York Times.* Catherine, Krupa, and a French girl named Annabel coming out of a near-empty restaurant onto deserted Elizabeth Street in bright dresses and heels. "The New Invincibles" read the headline, above an article about New York's young, rich set, impatient for life to return to normal. The picture had been raced around the Internet, had been picked up by news outlets all over the country. A splash of notoriety for Catherine, but that summer had been the last she'd spent in Krupa's circle.

"He also told me your mom died. Car accident. I mean, is that my business?"

"It's fine. I don't really mind—"

"And she left you all her money?"

"He said that?"

"Exactly the kind of dickish thing he does, right?" Frances paused. "But if you're all set up why work here?"

"I'm not—look, I don't really want to talk about it."

"If you change your mind, I'm a terrific listener."

Was she? Through the front window of a Korean restaurant next door, a dumpling chef stuffed ground pork into half moons of yellow dough. Catherine touched the bandage on her lower back. She'd changed it inexpertly the night before, examined the tiny swollen seam, no larger than a hyphen, and the tight stack of black stitches. The tape was already peeling. The area under the bandage throbbed. She pulled her hand away; she couldn't tell Frances about it, so why wonder?

She experienced a phantom whiff of her musty sheets. The fever had been so bad that she couldn't bear the shower. The pillows had felt like boulders. Salvos of pain shot upward from her gut. She'd called the clinic in a panic. "Totally normal," said the nurse. "It's the priming process Dr. Robeson told you about. Take fluids; let it run its course." So she'd been homebound and alone, and the pain got so intense she curled fetal in her bed, her forehead on her knees, thinking about dying, thinking—she couldn't stop herself—about her mother trapped in the crushed car, pinned there and bleeding.

Eventually the fever broke and vanished. She'd suddenly felt fine, just light-headed from lack of food.

"You're going to be sorry you hurried," Frances said as she stubbed the cigarette out and followed Catherine through the glass doors into a tiled lobby, the floor stained from a coffee spill. At the elevator Catherine thumbed 18. The elevator dinged open. "Sammy's not big on break time."

Catherine focused her attention on the greasy inspection certificate in a battered frame. The date was smudged. Frances picked at the elevator car's wood veneer and checked herself in the auburn-tinted mirror.

Catherine did the same. She was taller and slimmer than Frances, but the girl was sexier by a mile, in a boatneck top, snug jeans, and sandals. Incredible breasts too. And nothing fired Catherine's insecurities like a good set of breasts.

Their eyes met in the mirror.

"It's weirdly flattering, right? Something about the tint."

Catherine let herself laugh—not what she'd been thinking. She watched the lights rise through the seam between the elevator doors and tried to ease her heart rate down. She'd fainted twice yesterday, standing up out of a chair or the bed, discovering herself on the floor. She was determined not to faint today. "You're in school?" she asked Frances.

Frances shook her head. "Not since I coughed on a couple of campus police. Just to mess with them, but it only got me suspended. They'll never throw me out. Dad gives too much money to the place."

The elevator dinged. The doors slid open.

"The other girls there?" Frances shook her head. "Miss Hollins never turned away a paying applicant. I begged to go to Stamford High, but Dad's way too big of a Republican to let that happen."

They approached a reinforced steel door without a company sign or logo, just a cracked plastic button beside the frame and a dead-looking lipstick camera mounted at the ceiling. Frances pressed the button, took the metal knob in two hands, and seconds later, at a startlingly loud buzz, threw her weight to swing the door open.

Stained carpet led down a dingy hallway. Plastic-shaded fluorescents threw a waxy light over potted cacti lined up on the floor. "These are all Mercer's," Frances said. "What kind of freak collects cactuses? Cacti. Whatever." She nodded at a sprawl of fingerlike protuberances in a ceramic pot. "That one shoots needles if you get too close." Catherine ran her shoulder along the wall, keeping her distance. The carpet was worn through to the stone floor; the acoustic-tile buckled above her head. Catherine followed Frances around a bookcase stuffed with men's neckties, bottles of cologne, tubes of creams and shampoos. Diving watches, boxes of golf balls, squash rackets, men's dress shoes.

"All these companies think we'll recommend their crap to members," Frances said, lowering her voice. "Mostly guy stuff, but still— freebies'd be a perk if Sammy let us have any of it. But she's got control issues. Take, like, a cuff link and she's threatening to fire you."

Two empty offices opened off the hall, both crammed with shipping boxes and taped shopping bags with messenger labels. "I tell Mercer to buck up morale by making Samantha share the wealth, but he won't tell her what to do. He's like, 'Did *you* go to Wharton?'" She put a hand on her arm, physical contact Catherine felt grateful for. "Tell her you like her shoes. She's got a thing about shoes."

They came to a large room overlooking the street, with a dozen workstations laid out in a grid. The employees were all young women, all seated in front of terminals, a few of them speaking quietly into earpieces. Several glanced at Catherine—but not one of them smiled. Frances didn't acknowledge anyone in the room, just swung right, stepping around a low dividing line of filing drawers into a section furnished with a cracked leather armchair, a paddle-leaf cactus plant, and a standing halogen lamp. Near the window, a large polished-wood desk; its occupant had her back turned to them. Frances threw herself into the armchair and pulled out a magazine—one of the new survivalist glossies—half-buried in the cushion.

Samantha wore black eyeliner, bright red lipstick, Buddy Holly glasses in tortoiseshell, a ratty gray sweater, and crucifix earrings. Streaks of tangerine ran through her brown hair. Catherine would have guessed late thirties but the makeup made it hard to tell. Samantha swiveled a quarter turn in her chair but kept her eyes on her screen as she typed with her fingernails and made a sympathetic humming sound. She acknowledged Catherine by pointing at her blinking wireless earpiece and gesturing at her to wait.

"Petit St. Vincent's lovely but not in July." Her accent was . . . English? Australian? "Punta del Este? Nice villa there. Or Namibia. Yes—perfectly safe in Namibia."

Frances turned the pages lengthwise, opening up gatefolds, letting subscription cards flutter to the floor.

"We'll put our thinking caps on and one of the girls will be in touch." She touched her earpiece; rattled her watch, a man's diver model, like one of those Catherine had seen on the bookshelf; and swung around in her chair.

"Thinking cap means she doesn't know," said Frances. "Means she's got to call Mercer for advice."

"Good morning, Frances," Samantha said—startling Catherine. The accent had vanished. "To your desk, please."

Frances stretched her arms, performing an exaggerated yawn.

"Now." Samantha mouse-clicked twice. "Just sent you a load of MRs."

Frances rolled her eyes and stood. "I don't *need* to be here."

"Tell it to Mercer." Samantha pushed back from her desk and faced Catherine from her chair. Silver dog tags hung around her neck.

"I like your shoes," Catherine said, glancing at them: three-inch heels with ribbony straps.

"You're late," Samantha said. "Mr. Tramway said you were reliable. So prove it."

Catherine nodded.

"If you're late someone can't leave. We have night shifts here too, which I'm sure Mercer told you."

"He didn't explain much, actually." She paused. "*Richard* Tramway?"

Samantha looked at her more closely. The phone rang. "Laura?" she said.

From across the room Catherine heard a girl's voice greet the caller. Samantha stood and gestured for Catherine to follow her. "Mercer does the hiring but I get to do the firing," she said as they crossed the office to a workstation, backed almost to the wall.

"Understood," Catherine said as simply as she could. She felt foolish in her sensible sweater, blouse, and pants. The other girls, only a few of whom glanced up from their screens as she went by, had on loose sweats and old jeans. A Japanese girl in pigtails seemed to be wearing pajamas.

When Catherine sat down, her sight lines were cut to the keyboard, the screen, her phone.

Samantha rolled a chair over and showed her how to log in and view her Member Request queue. "Click open. See the request field? See the client history? Look for a note from me with instructions in this box here. Mr. Lin wants tickets to São Paulo, then a hotel with a vapor-sealed room. Also, helicopter charter." Samantha showed Catherine the suppliers, access codes, and account numbers to use.

"Looks pretty simple," Catherine said, even though it didn't.

"It's monkey work. Mercer should send me actual monkeys, just to see." Behind her glasses, Samantha's eyes turned soft for a moment, almost pitying. "Not what you went to college for, huh?"

"It'll be fine," Catherine said as brightly as she could, hearing one of the girls naming dates through her headpiece, another speaking Spanish. Below it all was the faint hum of the air-conditioning.

Samantha nodded. "MRs come in twenty-four hours and we promise a quick response. So check the time stamp and keep pace. If you need to call a restaurant or hotel say you're from Pursuit, but never explain who we are. The good places know. Eventually, there might be an errand or two I need you to run, but for now let's not stretch your talent." Samantha faked a smile and stood to leave her.

"Aren't there . . . ," Catherine said, her voice as low as she could make it. "Are there any forms I need to sign?"

"Top drawer on the left. Mercer's handling your benefit package, so ask him about that. He told you the pay?"

Catherine nodded, opened the drawer, and pulled out a folder. Inside were tax forms and what looked like a confidentiality agreement.

"It's what we can afford. Never use a client's name outside the office. Actually, I prefer you not tell people what you do at all."

"Sorry—what did you say about my benefits?"

"There's a new plan. I don't know anything about it," Samantha said, and turned abruptly toward her desk, her crucifix earrings knocking against her neck. Catherine heard a girl say, "How was Marrakech, Mr. Kulke?"

On Catherine's screen: a window with a column of blinking icons. She clicked on one and saw fields for a member name and membership number, and an instruction box with the words: "limo Gatwick." The needling gnats, the flashlights, were back in her vision.

Catherine dug her teeth into her lip. She settled uncomfortably against the seat back and took Tylenol from a tube of them in her bag. She rolled away from her desk looking for a water cooler.

Frances whistled under her breath. Pushing her own chair back from her cubicle into Catherine's line of sight, she pulled a trigger at the side of her head.

7

Frances made only occasional appearances at the office over the following month, and Catherine began to miss her whenever she wasn't there. Without Frances to provoke Samantha with complaints about the ambient temperature or the quality of the coffee in the machine, the room was as cowed and quiet as high school detention. And the work was like data entry—at least in the travel department, where a few mouse-clicks and keystrokes got members whatever they wanted: a pair of tickets to Kuala Lumpur, such-and-such Mustique villa for the month of September, a McLaren for a driving tour of Cornwall. Veteran girls fielded the calls, triaged the requests that pinged in, wrote them into formal MRs, and sent them to the room's loose departments: travel, restaurants and clubs, party planning, special requests (Frances: "Prostitutes"). "Your job is fulfillment," was how Samantha had explained the system on that first day, which already felt like last year. The line felt like a cruel joke.

The chair made Catherine's butt go numb and she developed a low-grade headache staring at a screen all day. She killed time listening to Samantha's fake accent, listening to her discuss the merits of such-and-such yacht club or an out-of-the-way brasserie, a new cocktail lounge in Istanbul where a biosecurity team conducted thermal scans at the door. She couldn't help thinking that not so long ago, Catherine might reasonably have expected Krupa to fly her to Istanbul; she might have sailed into that very yacht club in Corsica.

No, stop it, Catherine thought. She couldn't confidently say that Krupa had even liked her all that much. "Toilet princess" wasn't, after all, that chummy a nickname. She could be quite cutting too: Coming out of a dressing room at Jeffrey, wearing a printed silk dress, Catherine had received from Krupa an unsparing head-to-toe assessment and a quick head shake. "Definitely not," she said, lounging on the store's padded bench. "You don't fill it out." That was true, and Catherine certainly couldn't afford it, but she could still remember passing her overtaxed Visa to the salesgirl in a mood of hurt defiance. And then hurrying to catch up with Krupa, who was already on her way out onto Fourteenth Street.

Catherine's vision went double on the lunar glow of a ticket request screen. She'd gotten her spending habits from her mother. As a girl, Catherine used to stumble across one of April's discarded itineraries or spin the globe in the library and stop it with her finger and wonder, aggrievedly, if that exotic place was where April was conducting one of her shopping sprees. Now, pinned down in her cubicle, Catherine upbraided herself: *What a scold I was*. Catherine would have been right beside her if she'd been invited. She was trying not to think about April, nor how straitened and solitary her life had become since her death, how little effort Catherine put into making new friends. Or dating. She'd run Internet searches on a few of the Pursuit members' names. The usual wealthy types: men in their thirties and forties, from investment houses or hedge funds. The rich looked like they always looked. They'd never been her type before, but she couldn't help but admire how unabashed these men seemed. How thrillingly specific their lives were. They wanted a *certain* gambling suite in Macau. An *exact* tee time in Bermuda.

And yet there seemed zero hope of meeting any of them— Pursuit members never visited this office. Nor, for that matter, did

Mercer. Not one word from him since he'd sent her an insurance form to fill out.

Catherine barely spoke to anyone. The MRs poured in too hard and fast for office chitchat, for water-cooler gossip, and Catherine had the briefest exchanges in the ladies' room or in the hallway with her coworkers. The only event that disrupted the hours of her shift was the periodic delivery of boxes and shopping bags, all of which Samantha promptly tucked away in one of the two offices off the hall. When she wasn't doing that, Samantha was apologizing for delays to members on the phone. She fired paper clips off rubber bands at girls who lingered by the coffee machine. All-points text balloons would pop up on Catherine's screen:

>>Keep pace!

>>I can mirror your screens. Personal internet use is a firing offense!

"Is that a promise?" Catherine said aloud. None of the other girls around her laughed.

How long could she stick this out? And when would Mercer get her involved in whatever he'd said he was working on? *We'll have fun*, he'd said. She reminded herself that she still had credit card debt and that this job was the only stable thing in her life—but then wondered what was so great about stability.

Another text balloon appeared on Catherine's screen:

>>Duval, shut that browser window now.

Catherine let her eyes linger on the Web page she'd been reading, Acetor's "About Us" section, and did as she was told.

Didn't matter; she'd committed the website's high points to memory. Acetor was a Cambridge, Massachusetts–based medical device firm with a focus on micro-pacemakers; nothing on the site about TX immunity, though according to a single paragraph at the bottom of the company history page, Acetor's latest research was in "counterpandemic solutions." Those were two words worth putting into a search window when she got home, she thought. But she knew how depressed she'd feel stepping through the door of her apartment, how incapable of anything more ambitious than pouring herself a glass of Patrón, spreading peanut butter on crackers, watching TV, and going to bed.

She had called Robeson's office on her lunch break to ask for copies of the NDA and release forms she'd signed, intending to really read them this time. The nurse who answered asked if the stitches had dissolved (they had) and if Catherine had any pain. A little soreness, she said, but otherwise no. Dr. Robeson was on vacation, the nurse said, and would speak with her on his return.

She should have been relieved. Immune or not, she'd been to Dr. Cohen's since the surgery, and her swab had come up negative for TX. The gizmo in her back was working? Impossible to know. *Swabs can be inconclusive.* She felt as healthy as she'd ever felt. There were times she could forget the thing was even there.

8

Outside Catherine's bedroom window, through a cloud of building exhaust, a rooftop LCD billboard promoted discounted flights to Mexico City, Rio, Buenos Aires.

Wouldn't that be nice, she thought. She was lying in bed after another long, self-annihilating day at Pursuit, with a lease renewal from her landlord announcing a 30 percent rate hike flattened on her chest—a nasty surprise she'd found slid under her door.

Catherine stood, tossed the letter from her landlord away—she couldn't swing the increase on her Pursuit salary—and hunted in her closet for the silk dress, the one she'd bought at Jeffrey with Krupa. She tore it free of its dry cleaner plastic and wire hanger, took off her jeans and shirt, and stepped into it. Sure it was loose on top, but god, the cool kiss of the silk on her skin.

Zipping up the back, her fingers brushed against the swollen red seam of her scar. She pushed on the puffy skin, feeling for the edge of something hard beneath.

Catherine imagined what her father would say: "Tracking device. Tiny microphone. The government can hear us *right now*."

In the kitchen she slid the squat glass bottle of Patrón out of the cabinet. She gauged how much was left—this stuff was expensive, but a hot swallow or two really lifted her mood. Scanning the living room floor, half-wishing the mouse would appear, she uncorked the bottle and poured. "To immunity," she said, toasting the dusty baseboard.

Then she grabbed her bag, dropped her phone into it, and slipped on some flats, knowing the alcohol would make an evening walk through the neighborhood feel warm and dreamy. She could pretend that Mercer had actually meant what he said: *I need someone with poise.* That he might call and tell her that again.

She cut left out of her building to avoid being held up by a temperature-check station DOH police had set up on her corner (white van double-parked at the curb, folding table with thermal scanners). She turned onto Grove, passing a crowded bistro and a neighborhood German beer hall. News of TX outbreaks—anywhere, even halfway across the world—emptied places like this for days, but it never took long for them to fill up again. This was the pattern, well established over the last two years. Another right turn and then left and she was on the corridor of Christopher Street—also full of people. Some wore masks, but most didn't, or kept them slung around their necks. Taxis were jammed up, honking. Ahead of her, the sun dropped behind the high-rises of Jersey City. Color spread across the dark bowl of sky. Just four blocks that way, west of Greenwich Street, everything emptied out. The two to three blocks paralleling the West Side Highway had turned into a strip of abandoned condo towers, defunct car repair shops, and vacant warehouses. Two years ago, the National Guard had used Circle Line ships, Water Taxis, and ferries to carry the sick and dying off Manhattan, transporting them across the Hudson to Jersey City and on to Newark quarantine. The guard commandeered Hudson River Park for this purpose, from Battery Park City to Forty-Second Street. She remembered losing hours watching the footage on her TV: soldiers with riot shields and respirator helmets herding sick New Yorkers behind yellow tape, people leaping off ships—spotlights tracking them through intersecting wakes. The networks started by blurring faces, but then they gave that up. You searched the screen for someone you knew.

Property values along the river had plummeted. Businesses

relocated. The concern was that the government could take these streets over again if there was another sustained outbreak. The High Line was still an attraction but what you looked at was depressing: FOR LEASE signs where there had once been boutiques and art galleries. Luxury condo towers that stood empty except for security teams hired to keep out squatters. Garbage everywhere and men with carts hunting through it.

As Catherine felt the tequila start to thrum inside her, she thought of her mother, how glorious April's twenties had been here in Manhattan, drinking cocktails at the Odeon and the Surf Club, dating a Spanish prince. She'd never really left, even after moving to Richmond, always keeping a Manhattan apartment to escape to.

Catherine had once seen the inside of one of these places. Senior year in high school. An unannounced Saturday night visit. Catherine had decided to surprise her mother because April had been away for three solid months (a record) and because Catherine was tired of sharing a house with her father without knowing if her parents had finally separated or if this was just a new variety of matrimonial stalemate. Jack wasn't saying—though he did, when asked, give Catherine her mother's Fifth Avenue address. At which point Catherine put herself on the Northeast Regional to Penn Station, taken a cab to Seventy-Sixth and Fifth, and breezed past the doorman, saying as haughtily as she could that she was April Mayville's daughter. Up on the seventeenth floor she stepped into her mother's apartment, which was filled with soft Persian rugs and antique furniture, no pictures of Catherine or her dad anywhere. Two huge windows framed a glittery view of the park. Standing at the stove was a man in his fifties—dark hair, silver stubble, a dimpled chin—stirring something exotic-smelling in a pot. Beside him her mother had on these mortifyingly sexy leather pants and some kind of clingy top, sipping white wine, showing not the slightest sign of shock or annoyance at her daughter's appearance. She merely gave Catherine an amused grin and introduced her. Marcel was a real estate developer from Lebanon, slight and slim and very well dressed beneath the apron in dark gray suit pants and an immaculate white shirt. He poured Catherine a glass of wine.

"You knew I was coming," Catherine said when Marcel had excused himself to take a phone call.

April nodded. Jack had called to warn her. "And it's a good thing since Marcel and I had opera tickets. We wouldn't even have *been* here."

"You're living in New York full-time? You're divorcing Dad? I'm just trying to, like, get clarity on certain things."

April seemed puzzled by the interrogation. "I find it extremely liberating not knowing what I'll be doing tomorrow or the day after."

Marcel came back into the living room and gravely placed his phone on an end table.

"Please don't say anything gloomy," April told him.

"Just business," he said, and put his hand on April's arm and let his fingers trail up to the crook of her elbow.

"We got you a room at the Peninsula," April said. "I know you came all this way to play chaperone, but there's absolutely nowhere for you to *sleep*."

Catherine heard the hint of anger in her mother's voice, caught Marcel's close scrutiny—he was fully checking Catherine out—and paid attention to how both of these things pleased her. She finished her glass.

Catherine had been drunk and stoned with her field hockey teammates. She knew she liked the plummeting sensation of letting herself go. She watched her mother drink glass after glass, and noticed how her demeanor slipped from amused to bored to sleepy. Marcel filled the silence around the small dining table with talk about Middle Eastern politics and meetings he would be having at the UN and his development vision for Beirut's beachfront. April left the table on wobbly, wine-drunk legs to stretch out on the sofa; Catherine stacked the dishes in the sink, filled it with soapy water; and Marcel put on some traditional Lebanese music. April's eyes were closing and her shoes were off, and when Marcel invited Catherine to dance, she thought: *Why not?*

How assertively Marcel led her! How exciting the jittery, forbidden feeling of standing so close to him! Right there in the middle of the living room, his hands on her hips. She remembered noting how heavy his eyebrows were, how perfect and unblemished his coffee-colored skin. She remembered the noisy, nervous breath she'd let out when he slipped his hands under her sweater. Her mother's eyes were closed and she was breathing heavily. She looked old, slack mouthed, the veins in her ankles showing.

The music ended and Marcel kissed her good night—his breath smelled like raisins. He walked her to the door and they kissed again, for a long time. Finally, she broke away, whispered good night, and hurried to the elevator, her heart thudding in her chest. At the Peninsula, her room was huge and immaculate, and she took a bath in the marble tub, dried herself with one of the impossibly plush towels, and stood naked in the broad bathroom mirror. Her body, glistening and lean, seemed to her, for the first time, irresistibly sexy. She was seventeen years old.

A half block from Greenwich was a dive bar, with its bank of pinball machines and rave-y thump. Catherine considered going in for another drink—but only a few lonely-looking gay men sat on stools, enduring the music. Gnawed-clean chicken bones were scattered around on the sidewalk. Bolted to a nearby street sign and lit by a big blue light was an NYC Emergency Phone, its case standing open, the receiver hanging off its cradle.

Thoughts of Marcel made her bold. She pushed ahead, past the bar, past a windowless porn emporium, wanting a walk, wanting to get away from the familiar streets around her building. People went jogging along the river—it wasn't *so* dangerous. Plus the evening was pleasant and warm, and there was no one in her immediate vicinity to be on guard against. She passed maintenance garages and one plain-faced storefront with a black mirrored door, wondering if she was being unwise. A nightclub, she guessed from the faint pulse of bass underneath the sidewalk. On the corner of the narrow lane called Weehawken two men huddled over a campfire; she felt the heat on the side of her face as she passed. Something wet struck the sidewalk near her feet and Catherine let out a little yelp, realizing she'd been spat at. "Don't be 'fraid," wheezed one of the men by the fire. He was sitting on an overturned plastic can, his face shadowed by the brim of his baseball hat. "We don't bite," he said, clicking his teeth together.

The light was green, so she ran across the six lanes of stopped West Side Highway traffic, blood pulsing in her hands and feet. Trash and broken glass littered what used to be the bike path, and the plaza and pier were spotted with tents and cardboard lean-tos. To the south were the ventilation towers for the PATH and the hulk of Pier 40, jutting fatly over the water. The breeze kicked up, sweeping a heavy, fetid smell down from the tents to where she stood.

She'd keep to the path, go a block or two and loop back on Morton or Clarkson to avoid the men with the campfire. But almost immediately she stopped. A group of kids were in the bike lane, skateboarders doing tricks against concrete curbs. They wore torn jeans and baggy T-shirts. Tough-looking kids, with shaved scalps and tattoos.

Her phone vibrated in her pocket: a call coming in, that very moment. She nearly dropped it reading the name on the blue screen.

"Mercer," she said.

"What are you doing right now?"

"Out for a walk," she said as brightly as she could. She'd at-tracted the kids' notice. She turned around and headed for the crosswalk at Charles Street.

"You wouldn't be in the mood for a sort of . . . party? There's someone I'd like to introduce you to."

She looked down at herself—the bright hem of her dress, her battered flats. "When?"

"That's the thing: how quickly can you get to my office?"

She hurried but missed the light. Cars shot through, inches from the broken curb, lifting her hair. The three glass-clad hulks across the street were dead dark. "Half hour?" She heard the grinding wheels of a skateboard behind her.

"Hey." She turned and it was one of the kids, his lip dimpled in the fleshy center by a silver ring.

"Hang on," she told Mercer.

The kid came closer. She cocked her arm, the hand holding the phone, and he laughed. He held up his skateboard as a shield. "Gonna throw your phone at me?"

No, she wasn't. She put it back to her ear. "Mercer?" But he had already hung up.

She retreated a step until she was pinned against the traffic. The kid balanced the board on his head. "Got any money on you?" he asked casually, as if the question had just come to him. His friends were coming over as well.

Catherine shook her head.

The kid pulled something—a small hunting knife—out of the back pocket of his jeans.

"Leave me alone," she said, but the kid kept closing on her. Quickly, barely thinking, she picked up a broken piece of curb and threw it at him. Her aim was off, but he fell down trying to spin clear. His friends laughed.

In an instant he was back on his feet. There was a gap in the rushing cars—and Catherine sprinted through to the median, side-lit by swelling headlights.

9

She brushed her face with powder and pocketed a tube of lip gloss—and steadied herself with another swallow of tequila. Her adrenaline was up. She kept seeing herself with that chunk of concrete, except she hit the kid in the chest, felling him like a domino. The whole encounter seemed like the kind of story she might have told her mother, that her mother might have enjoyed. And now Catherine had a party to go to, which she would have liked too. She flew down the steps of her building and out the front door. The temperature-check station was gone, so she turned right and then went over to Seventh Avenue. There were hand-sanitizing stations everywhere—new ones—bolted to parking signs and bus kiosks. Vitamin-drink vendors advertising immunity shakes pushed their carts along the sidewalk. She made her way past them, east to Fifth, then up to Fourteenth Street. A fifteen-minute walk. And then the Pursuit building was dead ahead, the fourth floor glowing with a belt of white light. She checked the time on her phone. Not so late.

She pressed 4 on the keypad, as she'd done on that Tuesday morning a month ago, and smiled into the beady eye of the surveillance camera. Would any of the other girls from the office be there? She smoothed her hair and checked her breath in a cupped hand.

The door buzzed and in she went. Somebody's perfume lingered inside the elevator cab. She pressed the button for four and practiced casual hellos as the floors dinged past.

"Hey, hey! *So* glad you're here." It was Frances—and only Frances—smelling ripely of the perfume from the elevator, smiling at her out of a lopsided mouth, her lower lip bulging on one side. She wore a loose men's dress shirt knotted at the waist above a black skirt and held a champagne glass in her left hand and a bottle of Heineken in her right. The office looked empty behind her.

"Want a drink?" Frances asked. "They're not here yet."

"Who isn't? Yes," said Catherine.

Frances held the beer bottle up to her lips and spat daintily into it.

The space was even emptier than before—the neon Pursuit sign had been removed from the gray-painted wall, leaving a pattern of drill holes and dangling wires. Potted cacti had appeared on the conference table: a few comically bulbous, a few giants, and a cluster of miniatures, furred with purple needles. "He interviewed you here, right?" Frances asked, leading her around the folding screen that separated Mercer's office.

Catherine nodded. A black umbrella and a wooden coat hanger were hooked on the back of the screen. The panel that concealed a shelf of glasses and a mini fridge stood open; there was a door she hadn't seen before, at the far end of the daybed, revealing a full setup: tiled bathroom, glassed-in shower, bath towel slumped over a rod. Frances opened the mini fridge and smoothly poured Catherine a glass of champagne.

"*Salud*," she said, handing it over with a flourish.

"What's with your lip?"

She spat again into the beer bottle. "Bandits. The loose stuff gets everywhere. I'm trying to quit smoking." She sipped from her glass. "You don't have to make a *face*."

Catherine took in a mouthful of her champagne, wishing it were something stronger. She dropped her bag on the floor and settled on the daybed.

"Wow, god, cute," Frances said, rolling the glass against her mouth, indicating Catherine's dress.

"Oh," Catherine said, blushing. "Thanks."

"I barely have any clothes here in the city. But going home means dealing with my parents."

"Where's this party supposed to be?" Catherine asked.

"Dunno. Mercer just told me to get my ass up here on the double. He likes to think he can order me around. And now where is he?" Eagerness suddenly swept over her face. "There's this guy he's bringing."

Catherine nodded her head. "He mentioned someone he wanted me to meet."

"*You* to meet?"

Catherine shrugged. That's what he'd said.

Frances sniffed the air near Catherine. "You smell like booze."

She smiled. "Tough week."

"Tell me."

"Nope." But Frances was staring at her so intently Catherine felt she had to say something. "My landlord is hiking the rent."

"So move in with me," Frances said simply. "Mercer's never around. There's tons of space. Soho. Two floors. Kind of amazing windows."

"You're living with Mercer?"

"Until Dad's SWAT team arrives. Laird's there too. In the upstairs room, but we could get him to sleep on the sofa. Come on: fun. We'll max out Mercer's pay-per-view."

Not a real option, Catherine thought, though Frances's enthusiasm wasn't faked. Frances gave Mercer's chair a shove so that it thunked into the wooden desk. "Can't believe what I'm about to say, but sometimes I miss school. Crazy, right? Not the people, just sitting in class. I have this sort of good history teacher. I tell Mercer all sincerely and he's like, 'So, go back.'"

Catherine looked at her carefully, wondering what to say.

"Mercer loves doing that—messing with your head," Frances said. "When he graces you with his presence, that is. I've barely seen him in two weeks. It's enough to give a girl self-esteem issues."

Catherine drank more of her champagne. "We all have those."

"My mom sure does," Frances said brightly. "She thinks she's fat, and she is a little. But you can't help being a bit fat when you're her age. I told her."

"That was nice of you."

Frances retrieved the bottle from the fridge and filled Catherine's glass and hers, and then spat into her Heineken. "We're supposed to flirt with him. This guy. Not sure." She hesitated. "I'm glad you're coming."

Catherine smiled at her, feeling a motor inside her whir down to a lower gear.

There was the sound of the elevator doors and Mercer's voice in the outer office: "Anyone here?"

Frances put a finger to her lips, stepped behind the folding screen, and crouched, gripping the champagne bottle by the neck.

Laird entered Mercer's office without seeing Frances, scratching his ashy, dead-looking hair, that knife-blade tattoo running up the side of his neck. He wore the same royal-blue soccer jersey she'd seen him in before. TENNENT's across the front. "Hiya," he said to Catherine. "Long time no see."

Frances was still hiding. Catherine didn't know what to say. "You look nice," Mercer said to Catherine, coming in. So did he—healthier than a month before, the hollows in his face filled in. His cheeks had color and he'd let his hair get shaggy.

Frances let Mercer get near her and then sprang out of her crouch, bringing the champagne bottle down on him like a club, thudding high on the meaty part of his lifted arm. Mercer staggered.

Frances was breathing hard, delighted. Laird grabbed her and shoved her against the wall, a vein pulsing in his tattooed neck. He pried the bottle out of her grip and pinned her with the blunt base of it. Frances winced and then smiled. "Could have been a knife," she said. Mercer straightened up, his hand on his arm.

"Then I'd've stuck it in your fooking neck," Laird said.

He gave Frances another shove into the wall with the bottle—she let out a happy cry. "Point is you're a joke of a bodyguard," she said. Then she turned her attention on Mercer. "Sweetie, does it *hurt?*"

"You surprised me," was all Mercer said.

"I had the element of *surprise*, Laird," she said.

Laird moved the bottle off Frances and examined Catherine with new interest. "You're the decoy? Is that it?"

"Not—not intentionally, no," Catherine said.

Frances crossed to where Mercer stood and slid her hand around his waist, as if nothing had happened. "So where are we all going?" she asked. He stiffened, then nestled his hand in her hair, taking some of it in his fist.

"Don't do that again," he said, a dull whisper into her ear.

Frances—even with her head tipped up, held rigid—just rolled her eyes at Catherine. "He thinks he's scary," she said through her fat lip.

10

Mercer's Audi jostled over broken pavement, heading west on Nineteenth Street. "You drive like a maniac," Frances said, leaning forward in the backseat.

It was true. Laird violently alternated between gas and brake, gunning for any pedestrian who looked set to jaywalk. Catherine, next to Frances, gripped the root of her seat belt. "Where are we going?" she asked. Mercer ignored her, preoccupied by his phone, his fingers moving over the screen.

"And why won't you say anything about the guy?" Frances added, trying to read what he was typing.

"Someone I knew in college," Mercer said. "Sort of knew. Called Pursuit wanting to find out about this hardcore show."

"Is he cute?"

"Careful, Frances, you'll hurt my feelings."

"Oh sure," Frances said.

The foot traffic vanished as they proceeded west. When they reached Tenth Avenue, a light drizzle began to fall. The heavy brow of the High Line was ahead of them, a fenced car lot on the right. Across the avenue, the pavement sparkled with broken glass. The front of a gallery had been shattered, shards spread onto the street. Beyond this, a construction Dumpster was positioned halfway into the lane. Laird swung around it at speed. Catherine slid her hands under her legs. She thought of the kid ducking the concrete chunk

69

she'd thrown, spinning, falling—but she should stop congratulating herself. She'd gotten lucky. Stupid to go down to the river at night—and here she was again.

"I may need you to intimidate the pilot," Mercer said to Laird. "Try to get our rate down."

"Pilot?" Frances said.

Mercer dropped the phone into his lap with a satisfied sigh. Laird was waiting for an opening into the hurtling West Side Highway traffic. Laird found a gap and floored it, heading north, his race-car acceleration roiling Catherine's stomach. After about ten blocks, he slowed in the left lane, producing a chorus of horns behind them. Catherine's breath caught. There was a narrow break in the median ahead, also a NO LEFT TURN sign, and heavy traffic was coming from the other direction. Mercer stiff-armed the dash. "I hate when you do this."

"Plenty of room," Laird said right before he hammered the gas and threw the wheel.

11

From this distance, through the drizzle and chain-link fence, the helicopter looked appallingly fragile, the blades at droopy angles, its low, tapered nose inches from the ground. A pilot stood by the cabin, the wind off the Hudson flapping the loose nylon of his windbreaker. Mercer was out of the car in an instant, letting himself through the double gate in the fence. He jogged across the heliport's small parking area while Catherine, Frances, and Laird sat in the car.

"Look at that fooking thing," Laird said.

Catherine stared at the tatty helicopter. The black, sooty streaks near the tail rotor—were those burn marks? And was it even safe to go up in this rain? Mercer and the pilot retreated under the canopy of the small terminal hut. Something Mercer said made the pilot angry. Mercer pulled a fold of cash out of his wallet—but the pilot shook his head. He slapped the back of one hand into the palm of the other. Mercer let a minute pass, then spread his arms in a gesture of resignation and beckoned Laird to come over.

Laird got out of the car.

"You're about as intimidating as I am," Frances said.

But he *was* intimidating. The sinewy length of him, the tattoos, the jut of his chin. The pilot chopped the air a few times, but he was darting looks at Laird as he did so. Mercer slid his hands into the pockets of his pants and waited. The rain was coming in through Laird's open door. Catherine could feel it prickling her skin. Finally, the pilot shrugged. Mercer paid him and left the pilot counting the bills as he dragged open the gate in the fence.

Laird drove them through, parking the Audi adjacent to the terminal hut, out of view of the traffic. The whole facility looked abandoned to Catherine, no heliport staff, the tarmac cracked and sprouting weeds. Through the glass doors of the hut, a Coke machine threw a weak glow across old newspapers and coffee cups scattered on the floor.

"Howdy," deadpanned the pilot, rocking on his heels as Catherine, Frances, and Laird got out of the car. He was jowly, with a graying mustache and a stout gold watch latched tight on his wrist. He cracked his knuckles, measuring Laird and keeping his distance. "Waiting for one more, right?" Mercer ignored the question, his eyes on the whizzing highway. Laird gave the pilot a bulldog stare and the man muttered, "Shouldn't keep her sitting," twirled his finger around, indicating the weather, the authorities—Catherine wasn't sure—and moved off, toward the helicopter.

"This is safe, yeah?" Laird asked.

Mercer's answer was a nod in the direction of a small, powder-blue Ford, an electric two-seater, turning into the lot. Catherine shielded her eyes from the flare of its headlights as it pulled through the gate and parked beside Mercer's car. She could hear thumping and screaming from its speakers.

"Why's he drive a lawn mower?" Frances said as the music cut and a man in a tailored suit opened the door of the small car and stood. He had prematurely thinning dark hair, sloping shoulders, and the solid, plug-shaped body of a wrestler. Frances tipped her head as if trying to see him from a different angle.

There was something wrong with his face, Catherine realized. Swelling, especially under his left eye. Bruised, plum-colored knuckles peeked through the Ace bandage covering his right hand, which he held cupped to his stomach.

"Chad," Mercer said heartily. "In the flesh. It's been forever."

Chad responded with a noticeable lack of enthusiasm, lifting his chin, making the most of his height. "You're flying me somewhere?" he asked flatly, as if the idea held no appeal.

"And you're going to love it," Mercer said.

"Who's he?" Chad asked Mercer.

"My driver," Mercer said.

Chad let out a derisive laugh.

"I know, right?" Frances said. "Hi, I'm Frances. Since Mercer won't do the introductions."

Chad locked on Frances's breasts, ignoring the rest of her, and then turned to face Catherine. Rain drifted across the broken tarmac. Catherine thought of the parties in college, the way she'd submitted herself to the gazes of lushed-up guys. She'd liked it then, but this was different. Chad's interest wasn't sexual, not quite. It was an appraisal.

"You're the one whose mom died," he said. He aimed a key fob at his car and bleeped it locked. "You're lucky. I can't wait for my parents to die."

"That's a fooking heartless thing to say," Laird said. He pointed at Chad's injured hand. "Get that at the Sheetrock show?"

Chad headed toward the helicopter, where the double doors to the cabin were standing open. The pilot positioned a plastic footstool beneath them. Running lights glistened in the pooling tarmac.

"Friendly," Laird said.

Catherine gave Mercer a questioning look.

"You're not, like, obligated to come," he said.

"Oh, she's coming," Frances said. And Catherine let herself be taken by the arm.

12

Inside the helicopter, with the rotors beginning to thump, Laird rose out of his seat and pulled a tiny plastic envelope of cocaine from his pocket. Using the car key, he snorted two heaping portions.

Catherine watched Chad help himself, keying the coke up with his injured hand, then Mercer, who sat beside the pilot in front, the fat throttle jutting between his knees. Mercer offered the bag to Frances, who inexpertly dug out and, squeezing her eyes shut, sniffed up a small amount. Could be her first time, Catherine thought, and felt the helicopter roar and seesaw up off the pad. Catherine took her turn and bitter-aspirin flavor bloomed in her throat, the familiar elation climbing the back of her neck. In seconds, she'd shaken off whatever apprehension she'd been feeling. It was her first time in a helicopter, and she felt like cheering.

Outside the porthole window, the river, pocked with rain, dropped magically away. Mercer turned in his seat and pointed at the headsets on hooks near their heads. Catherine fitted hers over her ears and the microphone near her mouth. The headphones muffled the pounding of the rotor; in the speakers she could hear Frances's voice. "This thing's kind of a P-O-S," she said, rubbing her nose with one hand, picking at a loose seam in the cabin's upholstery with the other.

"She's Italian and fast as a mother." It was the pilot speaking defensively. He was working the pedals and the throttle, drifting them across the river. Wipers slapped the rain left and right across the windshield.

Tucked into a mesh pocket next to Catherine's seat was a worn-out brochure advertising Executive Helicopter Services. "VIP Manhattan Tours, Short-to-Mid-Range Executive Transport, Platinum Service."

"The Aga Khan has six," the pilot added.

"The Aga who?" Frances asked.

Chad blew out his cheeks and ran his tongue over his teeth.

Laird nodded grimly, a strained expression on his face. He'd fastened his seat belt, the only one of them to do so. "Glasgow coke. Not your average shite. Mate of mine flies it in."

Frances kicked Catherine's leg, a cartoon smile on her face. It was really hitting Catherine now. The spangled grid of the city shrunk in size and proportion as they rose. The helicopter banked and the cabin tilted thrillingly. "Fook me," Laird said over the headset.

Chad was the only problem. Catherine felt more stripped and exposed every time he turned his thick neck to take her in. *Ignore him*, Catherine thought, and succeeded, thanks to the view out the window and the crescendoing rush of the coke. Quarantine, a massive facility built on the Passaic River between Newark and Jersey City, was visible to the west: a sprawling concrete campus under a crescent of sodium light. Since it had been built, anyone who could afford to leave the area had gotten out. Newark was a mess, but even the towns like Bergen, Hoboken, and up into Teaneck and Fort Lee had turned dangerous.

Directly beneath them, Catherine could see shelters on the roofs of housing blocks, peeling billboards advertising year-old movies.

Frances leaned across Chad's lap, staring fixedly out the window too. In a small park, bodies huddled in the light of a trash can fire. Streetlights were out and not a single car moved on the blocks beneath them.

"Pretty," she said, pointing at Quarantine.

And it was, Catherine thought. The lights of the campus threw off a simmering tangerine haze. The main wards were supposedly empty, ready for the next TX outbreak. There were experimental clinics too where the DOH tested new drugs and treatments that never got written about. The place had armed guards, a high perimeter wall. Newark was the biggest quarantine in the country and it had the worst reputation. Two years ago, there had been reports of overcrowding, prison-style gangs, violence, and rape.

They banked north. The scenery turned to dense woods and the flickering lights of suburbs. These places were as they'd always been. The bedroom communities of Rockland County, and Westchester across the river. Then the Hudson River towns where wealthy New Yorkers still spent their weekends. Cars bulleted along the gray line of the Palisades parkway. The sky went gray to black as the lights of New York dropped behind them; the rain tapered off.

13

They hovered over a rural two-lane, whipping the roadside evergreens. Sawhorses and traffic cones marked off fifty yards of blacktop. Catherine felt the weight settle in her shoes as they landed. The rotors began to slow.

These were mountains north and west of the city. The Catskills? Catherine had never been up here. "That's the prison," Mercer had announced as they'd flown over the rain-streaked cell blocks, the damp, cratered exercise yards, the turreted walls and double rows of cyclone fencing. A decommissioned state penitentiary, Mercer said. And the neighboring town's main drag was a two-block strip of vinyl-sided storefronts, all dark except for a bar with neon beer signs in the window. One street lamp illuminated concentric tire marks in the intersection.

Stepping out of the helicopter on wobbly legs, letting Mercer take her by the forearm for balance, Catherine spotted the motel up a wooded rise. It looked like a roadside dive with a reception office and a line of numbered doors, a parking space in front of each. Except there was a towering roof deck built from fresh lumber at one end, rising high enough to crest the treetops. A sign mounted above the office read HIDEAWAY MOTEL and NO VACANCY. She rounded the helicopter, the rotors still tomahawking the air above her, her hair whipping around her face, and caught sight of a crowd down the road. Mostly men, a few women and teenage kids leaning against parked cars, pickup trucks and jeeps parked bumper to bumper on both shoulders. A pair of police cruisers with turning lights formed a barricade. The cops exited their vehicles and gave Mercer and Laird a wave.

"*Solid turnout,*" Mercer shouted in Chad's ear.

People were getting out of their cars and trucks to take a better look. Catherine counted at least twenty-five, maybe thirty men and women watching them. Some had their phones in their hands, taking pictures. Despite the warm weather, the men wore boots and jeans and quilted hunting vests or sweatshirts or canvas work jackets. The women had insulated gear on too. One man, drinking a beer, bearded and bearish in a New England Patriots sweatshirt, a pair of work goggles on his forehead, hawked and spat into the road.

The pilot popped open his hatch and climbed down. "I don't like the phones," he said, keeping his back to the crowd.

"We talked to Fritz about that, didn't we?" Mercer said to Laird.

Laird shrugged.

One of the bigger guys watching them crushed his beer can underneath his foot and began drumming the hood of his truck with it. The policeman by the sawhorses tipped his plastic-wrapped hat in Mercer's direction and his partner drew a shotgun from a rack inside the car.

14

The motel's heavy oak door admitted Catherine, Frances, Laird, Mercer, Chad, and the pilot to an enclosed, glass-walled vestibule. The small space rushed with a mini-cyclone of air and was ferociously lit by overhead lights. They stood squinting in a crowded huddle around a device on a stand, a panel the size and shape of a hardback book elevated four feet above the floor.

"Fritz is a bit of a germophobe, sorry," Mercer explained. "It was the reason he came up here in the first place. He made a pile at Goldman before people got sick." He bent slightly, directed a short exhale onto the sensor, and it lit with a friendly green light and a *ping*. "Do you invest in these guys?" he asked Chad. "Made by . . ." He checked the side of the machine.

"STH Systems," Chad said in a low voice, his first utterance in over a half hour. "No. False positives through the roof." He breathed on the scanner—*ping*—then thumped the thick glass wall with his knuckle. "Ballistic glass, though. There's money to be made in old-fashioned ballistic glass."

Frances and Catherine both blew on the scanner.

"Your turn," Laird said to the pilot.

He shook his head, unzipped his windbreaker. "Nothing illegal, you told me," he said to Mercer. "And already the drugs."

"I said no one gets *hurt*," Mercer said.

"Mate, do what you're fooking told," Laird said, shoving him from behind. The man lurched forward, catching himself with one hand on the machine. He gathered himself, glanced behind him, and blew on the panel. *Ping.*

The glass partition slid open and the overhead lights cut. The man meeting them on the other side looked like a drill sergeant: compact frame, hair shaved close to his scalp. He seemed about sixty and was tidy in his movements, calmly inspecting each of them in turn—studying Chad the longest. "Welcome to the HideAway," he finally said in a soft voice. The accent was German. "I'm Fritz."

Catherine took in the space behind him. It had been a motel lobby—wagon-wheel chandelier, vaulted acoustic-tile ceiling broken by skylights, cracked laminate flooring, the smell of old dust. To Catherine's left stood an antique walnut bar with scroll-carved edges, a tiered rack of glasses, and wainscoting. Some kind of renovation was under way. The wall dividing off the guest rooms had been knocked down, opening a long, railcarlike space, sparsely furnished with a pair of club chairs, a bench seat crudely hacked out of a tree trunk, and a mounted TV. Mismatched rugs covered the floor: a fluffy bearskin, a couple of deep-pile throws.

Catherine's attention stuck on the taxidermy collection. A stuffed fox leered at her from a low table; a moose's head grinned goofily from a trophy mount on the far wall; two rabbits flanked the TV on a ledge. A dozen pieces scattered throughout the space: teeth and claws and beady glass eyes and fur.

"What do you gentlemen drink?" Fritz asked, stepping toward the bar. "Mr. Paterno? Maybe just a Coke?"

"He knows my *name*?" the pilot said.

"He'd love a Coke," Mercer said, and Laird steered the pilot roughly to one of the club chairs and sat him down.

Fritz circled behind the bar and filled a glass from a soda gun, holding it carefully by the base, then handed it to Laird, who passed it on to the pilot. Fritz plucked a remote control from the top of some liquor bottles and cycled through channels to what looked like porn: two nude girls splashing each other in a kiddie pool.

The pilot slowly turned his head away from the screen. The girls smiled android smiles; their breasts were like molded plastic.

"And of course I know who you are, Mr. Bonafleur," Fritz said, speaking to Chad, replacing the remote and pumping sanitizer onto his hand. His consonants were precise, his voice pitched a little high.

"Can we get to whatever it is?" Chad asked.

"Show him," Mercer said. And Fritz promptly crouched below the bar.

"Bonafleur?" Frances said, her eyes wide and bright from the coke. "That's, like, the *gayest*—" She broke off.

Fritz was holding a pair of black pump-action shotguns with molded plastic stocks. He clunked them heavily onto the bar top—a sound that made Catherine jump. "Twelve-gauge riot guns," he said. "Use blunt-force plastic rounds. Health Department used them to enforce cordons during the worst of it." This came out *the vurst of it*. Fritz gave them all a tight smile. Then he pulled a bright orange cardboard ammunition box from beneath the bar, the words NON LETHAL in boldfaced capitals on its side.

"I don't get it," Frances said.

Someone had given the naked girls a beach ball. They lobbed it back and forth, laughing their silent laughter.

Horns started honking outside.

15

"Natives are restless," Mercer said, peering into the night through a pair of binoculars.

He turned the binoculars over to Catherine, who brought the locals down on the road into focus. They did look impatient—elbows cocked on hoods, more beer cans tossed into the road—waiting for whatever activity involved the barrel of fist-sized sandbags beside her, and the thick rubber cord, a kind of heavy-duty slingshot, anchored to two steel rods at one end of the platform.

They'd all, minus the pilot, assembled up on the motel's crow's nest, a couple of stories high and about fifty yards away from the road. To get up here, they'd climbed a ladder through a hatch to the roof of the motel and passed along a series of planked catwalks, Fritz talking the whole time about how there was nothing around for miles, how he'd put the word out through his local taxidermist about Mercer and his rich friends, real money if people came out, plastic ammunition so no one gets hurt. Don't worry about the police, he told Chad, who didn't look worried.

Now Fritz was arranging the guns and boxes of ammo near the railing. "Direct hits will knock a man down," he said. "But if you aim at the pavement you'll get a very nice scatter effect."

Through the binoculars Catherine saw that the crowd had grown—close to fifty people down there now. She passed the binoculars to Laird and retreated to where Frances was sitting, in one of two lounge chairs near the stairway, and rubbed her face with both hands. She decided she didn't want anything to do with what happened next. The weather had cleared; summer breezes sheeted down out of the night sky.

Chad took the gun Mercer was offering and attempted to work the pump action with his good hand, his left, bracing the stock against his knee. "Help me," he said to Frances.

"Please?" Frances asked.

Catherine took the rapidly depleting bag of cocaine and key from Laird.

"All right. A demonstration," Fritz said. He took a sandbag out of the oil drum, placed it in the leather cradle of the sling, and walked it backward.

Chad positioned Frances directly in front of him, backing her up to his chest so she could hold the gun. He hung his hurt hand over her shoulder, immobilizing her with it. "My neighbor Jeff?" Frances said to him. "His little brother launches water balloons into our yard with one of those."

Catherine settled and waited for the drug to work. She squeezed her burning nostrils and sniffed twice to get any residue up into her nasal cavity.

"I treated the rubber with chemicals to create pliability without diminishing strength," Fritz said to Mercer, grunting as he stretched the cords taut. "The result . . ." He gritted his teeth, struggled another step backward, and released. The rubber convulsed, snapping like live snakes across the shooting platform, the cradle smacking into the barrier rail on the other side. Catherine watched the sandbag follow a dark arc over the trees. "Is a much farther shot."

But the bag didn't make the road, seeming to stall in the breeze and dropping down through some branches. One of the locals whistled; another shouted encouragement. This was followed by a chorus of voices and the honking of a car horn.

"Little short, mate," Laird said.

"So we adjust the trajectory," Fritz said, telescoping the steel rods higher.

"The trajectory's not the problem," Laird said, jostling him out of the way. He loaded a sandbag into the cradle and walked it farther backward than Fritz had, showing little effort. He crouched to hold the cradle low and released.

The rubber snapped and the sandbag punched into the night air, sailing higher, farther. Catherine stood and saw it smack the road, scattering sand onto the wheelbase of a pickup truck. Two of the local men huddled over it and then waved others off.

"Looks good," Mercer said. He'd taken the other riot gun and had positioned himself at the railing.

The coke sent a shiver of adrenaline across Catherine's shoulder blades. She kept noticing how steady Mercer's mood was, how little he seemed to be bothered by the way Chad was squeezing Frances across the breasts. Mercer caught her looking at him and let out a half smile. He kept his body cheated toward hers. Out of his suit pocket came an enormous wad of bills.

16

It went this way: Fritz would take a fifty or a hundred from Mercer's roll of cash and rubber-band the bill to the sandbag. Laird would slingshot the weighted money over the trees. As soon as it landed, a group down on the road would go after it. Mercer and Chad would fire as many shots as possible, trying to keep them back. Mercer was good at this, shooting, sliding the grip, sending an empty cartridge somersaulting away. Chad, with his hurt hand, had more trouble. He could either work the grip or pull the trigger—not both. And Frances kept squirming away. Chad tried bracing the stock against her shoulder, pinning her to him, but it was an awkward operation. He'd get one shot off to Mercer's four before Fritz, watching the street through binoculars, lifted his arm.

"It's hard, right?" Mercer said, lowering the gun, a halo of gray smoke settling around him. "They come in quick."

"Ow," Frances said, waggling a finger in her ear.

Catherine's own ears were cottony with a dull ringing sound, and the pencil-lead smell of gun smoke filled her nose. People were getting hurt—they spun away when Mercer or Chad pulled their triggers, clutching an arm or leg—but within seconds whoever it was had shaken off the pain and was waving at the roof deck for the next round.

"Again," Chad said, swinging the gun with his good hand.

"Watch where you're pointing that fooking thing," Laird said.

Fritz offered Catherine the binoculars, and she took them. Catherine watched a man stuff wads of newspaper down his shirt; a woman with long, gray hair polished the lenses of a pair of work goggles with the hem of her dress. A boy—couldn't have been older than ten—held the top of a garbage can like a shield. "This is sick," she said, without conviction, as Laird loaded the slingshot again. The money-wrapped bag went up like a softball over the trees, and Mercer smoothly aimed his gun. Frances squirmed, trying to protect her ears and work Chad's trigger at the same time. Chad brought her closer, roughly jamming the butt of the gun into her thin shoulder to get her to stand still.

Catherine lifted the binoculars. The bag landed in a lit stretch of road. Shots detonated in Catherine's ear; puffs of dust blew up off the tarmac in her field of view. That was Mercer firing. Down below, a half circle of people moved as a group. Magnified, she could see a pair of big men and two women darting toward the cash-wrapped bag. They jumped back as Mercer's shots scuffed the pavement. When Mercer paused to reload, a woman hiked her sweatshirt up over her face and lunged the last twenty yards, ducking her head. Chad barked at Frances to pull the trigger. She did so while trying to cover one ear, leaning away, throwing off his aim.

Chad shoved her with his elbow and, backhanded, squeezed off a waist-level shot. Nearby leaves exploded from branches.

Perched on their car hoods, the police—who had been watching impassively—looked up.

"Touch high," Laird said.

"Easy, spaz," Frances said from where she lay on her butt.

Chad rounded on her, notching the gun into his armpit and managing to slide the grip one-handed.

"*Oi,*" Laird said, leaping between them. He tipped the gun to Chad's shoulder.

Chad's lips were a white line. Nobody spoke.

"It's extra if you want to shoot one of our own," Mercer said casually. Only Fritz smiled. Chad stared at Laird without blinking, then took two slow breaths. He looked down at his cupped, injured hand. "I need some—" he started, then addressed Mercer. "Some fucking Tylenol."

17

Fritz said he could do better than that. He had codeine in a first aid kit behind the bar. He set off along the catwalk to get it. "Cate's turn," Mercer said.

"Hey, I'm fine! Nobody worry about me!" Frances said. She'd seated herself on one of the lounge chairs, her arms crossed tightly against her chest.

Catherine took the gun from Mercer. It was surprisingly light and easy to lift, and warm on her palms and fingers. She wasn't going to shoot, she told herself, even as she crouched, opened the cardboard flap of the ammo box, and slid a red cylindrical cartridge into the magazine slot as she'd seen Mercer do. She was surprised how easily it went, sliding home as if magnetized, making an oily click. She tried gripping the knobby plastic slide, just for fun, and found it stiff, hard to move. She had to brace the stock against her hip and slide the grip with both hands. As it ratcheted down the barrel, she felt the mechanism inside, felt the cartridge sliding into its chamber. A loaded gun in her hands.

"Safety's by the trigger," Mercer said. Catherine looked, found a small red nubbin, and thumbed it flush. *Plastic rounds*, she thought. She aimed well away from anyone on the road, at an empty stretch of woods, and closed her eyes.

The recoil sent her staggering—a punch to her shoulder. "Ow," she said, opening her jaw against her ringing ears.

"Okay?" Mercer asked, amused. She nodded, standing upright, and he said, "Here." He guided her to the rail, moved the barrel toward the locals below them. "Lean into it," he said, and his hand found her elbow, where it steadied her aim. She nestled into him. "And get the butt snug."

Laird sent a sandbag strapped with a fifty high into the air, and, with Mercer's help, Catherine followed its flight along the barrel. She put the bead where the bag landed on the road, held her breath, and fired again, anticipating the kick better, absorbing it with her shoulder.

Had she hit anyone? People were moving around down there; it was hard to tell. She worked the slide and aimed at a woman, a blonde, moving in on the bag. Her finger found the trigger.

Thirty minutes later, the pilot was snoring in the armchair. The girls in the kiddie pool were gone. The TV was a solid blue screen.

Catherine sat in the other chair and curled into the cushion, wishing she could sleep. She heard more gunshots from upstairs, felt them vibrate in her stomach, and experienced, again, the recoil punch to her shoulder. She saw the woman she'd shot drop to her knees.

"Mercer says Chazza will make us all rich," Laird called over from the bar. He'd been sent down to collect a bottle of vodka and some glasses for the group.

"Great," Catherine said dully, and folded her hands together to keep them from vibrating. The woman she'd shot had gotten to her feet and limped away. And that had been that. Catherine had handed the gun off to Mercer, no longer having a good time. She joined Frances on the lounge chair. Eventually, the noise had driven her down the ladder and inside the hotel.

Laird offered her a shot of vodka.

"The coke?" Catherine asked.

"Upstairs."

She shrugged, not wanting to climb the ladder. "Get comfortable," Laird said, and drank her shot. "Plenty of ammo to get through."

Catherine tented a thin cotton blanket she'd found around her head and listened to Laird climb through the hatch one-handed, the glasses clinking against the vodka bottle he was carrying. She rubbed her face, saw Chad's elbow catch Frances in the jaw, and tried to think of nothing. She heard the pilot's heavy breath clog.

More time passed. It wasn't sleep—sleep was impossible—but she must have fallen into a shallow, drifting semiconsciousness because she missed Mercer's approach, didn't feel him standing over her, only became aware of him when he touched the tender skin of her lower back, his hand warm through her dress. She jolted upright.

Mercer put a finger to his lips. He crouched at the arm of the chair. He'd taken his jacket off, opened his shirt another button. A fireplace smell came off his skin: flint, gun smoke, ash. "There's just a tiny scar, right? And no pain at all when Robeson put it in. How's it feel?"

She looked around: just the pilot, still sleeping. "How's what feel?" she asked.

Mercer smiled. "It doesn't hurt, right?"

She shook her head.

"Immunity," Mercer said, close, focused on her expression. "What does *that* feel like?"

"It feels like I want to go home," she said.

Mercer laughed and nodded. "Well, too bad. We have a very happy boy. You looked good up there too. See the appeal?"

"Not really."

"Yes, you do."

At that moment Chad came heavily down the ladder. "You're out of coke," he said, damp hair plastered to his brow. Fritz trailed him, cradling the guns like firewood. "Out of cash too. Next time you'll need a lot more coke and cash."

THE LIMITS
OF BAD
BEHAVIOR

18

Over the next three weeks Mercer quietly spread the word about the HideAway to the Pursuit membership and the waiting list stacked up. Fritz doubled his arsenal of riot guns to four and laid in crates of ammo; Laird kept topping up his supply of cocaine, now a staple of the HideAway experience.

Laird and Mercer were flying to the Catskills every Thursday and Saturday night, but all was not well, according to Laird, because Chad had not been heard from. His investment dollars had not come through.

"As if he didn't have the time of his sad life," Laird said on a midmorning Sunday. Catherine, Frances, and Laird were reclining sleepily on leather sofas in Mercer's Spring Street apartment. The sunshine through the warehouse windows dimmed the TV screen and set Laird's crew cut aglow. He stank of cordite and sweat.

Frances kicked him. "Take a shower."

"Use mine," Catherine offered.

"*Yours*," Laird said. "Made herself at home, hasn't she?" This was gentle teasing. Laird had been courteous about Catherine's arrival. She'd displaced him from the second bedroom, but Laird said he didn't mind the sofa. He kept odd hours, constantly ferrying Mercer around or accompanying him upstate.

"Mercer's fooking gutted Chad hasn't called," Laird went on, unlacing his battered combat boots. "You can tell."

"*You* can tell," Frances said, standing up off the sofa and crossing to the kitchen. "The rest of us never see him. Anyone want a Bloody Mary?"

"Lager," Laird said.

"Sure," Catherine said. Before her lease ran out she'd called Mercer three times, texted him twice, and finally left a voice mail: "Frances invited me to move into your place for a little while. She says you have a guest room? Call me if it isn't okay. Just . . . call me anyway."

But he hadn't, so Catherine packed only essentials, toting garbage bags of books and old clothes to a thrift store, and when she showed up in a cab on Friday evening, Frances had mixed a celebratory pitcher of margaritas. "You're sure this is okay?" Catherine asked. Sprawled on the queen bed in the airy white box of a guest room, Frances just laughed. "Whatever, the place isn't even his." A loaner from some friend. White walled, sparely arranged rooms furnished with replica modernist seating, a kitchen with an elaborate espresso machine, a giant TV bolted the wall. Not a book or memento or family photo in sight.

What could Catherine do? Settle in, get through her work days at Pursuit, think about what they'd done up at the HideAway. She kept remembering the way she'd leaned into the gun, the way her conscience had disengaged. Her ears had rung for days; her shoulder had ached for a week. She also thought about Mercer's question: *How's it feel?* The implant still felt like nothing, and of course, she couldn't be sure she was immune—but she *did* find she wasn't thinking like she used to. She'd all but stopped disinfecting her hands. She never put a mask on. She'd called Robeson's office twice to schedule a follow-up appointment but was told by the nurse that Robeson was still on vacation and would call her on his return.

She doubted that. She wanted to talk to Mercer. He was the one who'd gotten her this thing. But he was never home. According to Laird, he spent all his time at the office on Fifth Avenue, going through the Pursuit membership files one by one, searching for a HideAway investor—even sleeping there most nights.

Except, how to explain the late-night noises she'd heard through the floor? The bed below shifting and rocking, Frances making shrill, pained-sounding cries, a loud and heavy thump, like someone falling to the floor.

Simple: Mercer wasn't spending *every* night at the office. He was coming in late and he and Frances were fucking. But Catherine couldn't bring herself to confirm this with Frances directly. She worried she'd come across as jealous. *Was* she jealous? That question opened a windy, empty space in her chest that she felt she might fall into.

"Why do we even need an investor?" Frances called over from the kitchen. "Aren't you charging enough?"

"'Cause the cops are fooking greedy," Laird said. More locals were coming out, he explained, which improved the atmosphere but also meant more police had to be bribed to work crowd control. Plus plastic ammunition was expensive. Popular as the HideAway was, the operation was bleeding company reserves.

Frances lobbed Laird a can of Carlsberg and sat down with her own freshly made cocktail, stirring it with a celery stick. It was the right rusty color—plenty of Worcestershire sauce.

"Where's mine?" Catherine asked.

"Whoops."

Laird aimed an invisible shotgun at Frances. "I tell Mercer he's got to go farther if he wants to get Chazza's attention. Let him fight one of the locals. Shoot them up close. Guy can't control his blood-lust. Plenty of fookers like him where I come from."

"Sounds nice," Frances replied.

"I told him this when we were up there," Laird went on. "'Chazza,' I said. 'The potential for profit flying rich punters to Scotland is fooking staggering. Get proper guns into their hands. Turn the lads on each other.' Didn't look like Mercer cared for the idea, to be honest."

19

"Why so modest?" Frances called through the bathroom door. "You've got a great body."

Standing in front of the mirror, stripped to her underwear, Catherine thought, *Not so bad.* Since getting Cytofit she'd even lost weight on her hips, the place it usually collected. She threw one shoulder toward the mirror and examined the freckles scattered across the backs of her thighs, the twin dimples above her butt, and finally, the implant scar—still red, still raised, but painless to the touch.

"It zips in the back," Frances said.

"It won't cover my butt," Catherine said, holding up the dress Frances had given her to try on, approximately the size of the hand towel beside the sink. She stepped into it, hitched it over her hips, zipped it up above the scar, and then tipped the last drops of Bloody Mary into her mouth.

The knob shook. "So what? Let me see."

Catherine unlocked the door. She hadn't come in here for modesty but to keep Frances from asking questions about the scar as she undressed. Catherine had never been a good liar, and Frances was disarming. Catherine had already told her more stories about her mother than she'd ever told anyone, but Frances kept saying April was no worse than a million moms. The world was a straightforward place if you wanted it to be. These ideas got Catherine talking about the accident, saying certain things aloud for the first time: "I sometimes think suicide," she'd said, and experienced, at the time, a chilly sort of thrill. Drinking too much and losing control of the car was never the most plausible scenario. April had been driving drunk her whole adult life. She used to think nothing of downing a bottle of wine and sliding behind the wheel. A lifetime of that and never a mishap—but then suddenly she hits a tree? Wet road, driving too fast, blood alcohol of 0.19 said the accident report, but couldn't there be another explanation? She knew her money had run out and felt a jolt to her conscience, an inkling of guilt for the years of neglect—

"Sort of a dramatic theory though, right?" Frances had interrupted. "I get it. You're relieved. I'd be too. You don't have to feel guilty."

"I'm not relieved," Catherine had said. "She told me she loved me the last time we talked. Which she pretty much never did."

"Time to move on."

And maybe it was. Catherine admitted this to herself as she stared into the bathroom mirror. Frances's dress was far more revealing than anything she owned, open in the back, loose in the bust. "Door's open."

Frances let herself in. Her lower lip bulged with Skoal. "Sexy," she confirmed, tugging the zipper the rest of the way up. "Told you all you needed was some better clothes."

To start dating again. Catherine had admitted to Frances how long it had been. Frances had finished mixing more Bloody Marys and said she'd give her something to wear. "How do you sit down?" Catherine asked her now, turning around, tugging the hem.

Frances set her empty glass on the bathroom counter, leaned over the sink, and spat into it. She ran the water and looked at Catherine with a serious expression.

"I'll know if you sleep with him."

"Who?"

"Mercer."

"Please," she said lightly. "Not my type."

"Liar."

"No interest. I swear on my mother's grave."

"You hated your mother."

Catherine shook her head, appalled at how hard she was blushing. "I never said hate. You weren't listening."

"Right, right. Yawn."

"Why don't you go see him instead of waiting around here?"

"Already did. Want to know what he told me?"

"You went to his *office*?"

"The other day. I threatened to go back to school. And he's all"—she did a baritone impression of Mercer—"'Stick around. You're critical to this whole operation.' I'm like, how? Give me a clue. So he writes down Chad's phone number." She lowered her voice as if someone might overhear. But there was only Laird, out of earshot downstairs. "I'm like, you want me to call and what? Mercer goes, 'He's in charge of half a billion. There's rich and then there's whatever he is.'" Frances paused and fist-rubbed her left eye. "As if . . . as if that's the whole reason . . . Forget it."

Catherine remembered being seventeen. She remembered watching girls on her field hockey team effortlessly draw the attention of pretty much any boy at school they wanted. Frances was like one of those girls: killer body, quick-witted; she *should* go back to school, surround herself with friends, go to parties, find a boy her age, do ordinary seventeen-year-old things. Where were her parents? Frances said they'd written her off, but Catherine found this hard to believe. Equally hard to believe were the tears collecting in Frances's eyes and what she was saying now, pushing her hair behind her ear: "C, you're like my only friend."

Frances was Catherine's only friend too, but she would never admit it. She thought about Maggie. She thought about Krupa. She still had Krupa's number buried in her phone. She should call to say hello.

"Why don't you come into work tomorrow?" Catherine said, not meeting Frances's gaze. "A day at the office might be good distraction."

"Sammy doesn't want me there. She said so."

"Okay, well look, don't take this the wrong way, but . . . maybe going to school isn't such a bad . . ."

Frances blinked a tear away. She spat into the sink again. "*Such* a liar," she said. "Take off the dress before you stretch it."

20

Catherine walked along clean and quiet streets to the subway at Prince. She passed a DOH mobile station, four officers standing around a windowless van, and one of them aimed a handheld thermal scanner at her chest. *Little higher, buddy*, she thought, picking up her pace.

Those things gave a pretty decent view through your clothes. And yet? The feeling wasn't altogether unpleasant. Was she really so desperate? The loneliness was gone—Laird and Frances had taken care of that—but her restlessness remained, a tremor down in the core of her. She wondered if it would ever go away or if she even wanted it to. She was still shaking off the dream from the night before: Phillip tearing her shirt open, kissing her neck, her breasts, and throwing her against the wall of her old apartment. An amazing feeling but also pure fantasy. Phillip had never come on so strongly the whole time she'd known him. Still, lying in bed in a twilight of sleep and wakefulness, her eyes closed, she could feel it: the impact, over and over again.

She could blame Frances's ridiculous dress, the sleek, new version of herself she'd seen in the mirror on Sunday. Or what Frances had said: *I'll know if you sleep with him.* As if that was a real possibility.

But it wasn't Mercer she wanted—or not only. She wanted more coke, another flight across the Hudson. Another turn with one of the guns. She stopped at the coffee cart on Broadway, and the broken-toothed Afghan smiled at her, spoon-tossed sugar into a cup, and dispensed her regular order—small black, sweet—from his battered kettle. She pressed her hands against the cardboard cup and moved away from the van's curling steam. She would spend the next eight hours knocking down her screen's blinking column of member requests, point and click, point and click, *monkey work*. The same routine five days a week. She felt like a plane circling an airport. And how excruciating to watch Pursuit members fire-hose their money around while her own bank account went *plink, plink, plink*.

The newsstand papers all carried headlines about a TX outbreak in a Baltimore child-care center. KIDDIE CARE HOT ZONE, screamed the *Post*. She read down the column: three children dead, four hundred in Maryland quarantine. No cases of immunity or resistance seen. The DOH was on full alert. It was the first American TX outbreak in months. Anyone with symptoms should declare themselves to their doctor or the nearest health center immediately, officials said. There'd be stepped-up health patrols all over the city.

She watched the mask seller do brisk business, selling polyester masks from a rigged length of PVC. Street vendor masks were cheap— the elastic bands snapped off and the fabric clotted with your breath— but still you bought them, because the subway was a crossfire of germs. The Jamaican was selling them as fast as he could, slipping masks off the pipe with his gloved right hand, passing them to commuters as they went down the subway steps. The man beckoned Catherine; she handed over her dollar but stuffed the mask in her bag. She wasn't going to wear it. Her days of suffocating in the subway were over. She still carried a lightweight microfiber mask, but that was old habit—as was the deep, pearl diver's breath she took at the top of the subway steps. Once she was down on the tiled platform, she found herself breathing normally. An R train clattered in and she stepped into the car, noticing the way other riders stared at her uncovered mouth.

She liked the way they gave her space. She took a seat and studied the latest DOH public service placards. A sick man at a blackjack table, eyes bloodshot, poker chip in one hand, wadded tissue in the other; THE HOUSE ALWAYS WINS. Then, below: REPORT SYMPTOMS; GET SCREENED; DON'T GAMBLE WITH TX. And the DOH shield. Scare tactics, her father would say. She heard his voice in her head: *They did it to us the first time and they'll do it again.*

She emerged at Herald Square into a logjam of cabs, their horns all going at once, feeling the sun on her face. When an oddly fresh city breeze blew past her, she took it in as if it were mountain air, weaving and sliding between parked cars and street signs along the narrow curb. Waiting to cross Broadway, she noticed a guy in a blue Yankees cap and a black T-shirt staring at her. Instantly, his eyes lost focus and he turned south, heading down the block.

Someone she knew? At the walk sign she crossed into a snarl of construction; the man had disappeared into the crowd of rush-hour pedestrians—almost all of them, she noticed, were wearing masks. The Baltimore thing had people on edge, she thought. Restaurants might even start emptying out. She plugged her ears against a sledgehammer. Workmen were scattered around a huddle of trucks. A temporary plywood barrier bottlenecked the sidewalk. Annoyed, Catherine considered looping north around the block to get to the office from Fifth Avenue, but that would make her later than she already was.

The plywood barrier went above Catherine's head. Through rough-sawed openings she could see sweating workmen in orange vests, the exposed guts of the street, the ancient pipes and cables, and black, oozing mud. A flash of blue light erupted from the rubble, settling a fantail of sparks onto a plastic tarp. Catherine trudged along behind a man in a suit, who clutched a briefcase to his chest. She kept her ears plugged against the sledgehammer racket; the burnt-toast smell made her hungry. Another blue flash erupted; Catherine heard a weird thrum in the air.

Someone pinched her hard from behind. She spun to confront whoever it was, but saw only a heavily made-up blonde in tight jeans giving Catherine an ugly look. Catherine spun again, slapping at a stinging pain in her back. She reached under her shirt. The scar was a smooth, slightly raised line. Something was happening beneath the skin, though—a filament spasm tripping through the center of her.

"You okay, lady?" That was the man in front of her. She'd stepped too close to him.

No. The bottleneck wasn't moving. A Con Ed truck was reversing into a service bay, a workman with an orange baton blocking progress. She felt the pinch again, not so painful, but she had to squeeze her eyes shut to avoid crying out. *Beep, beep, beep* went the truck. "Excuse me," Catherine said. "Sorry. Excuse me. I have to. . . . Sorry." She shoved through the crowd, pins and needles in her legs, causing a commotion, getting shoved back.

"Hold up, miss," the workman said, his hand out, but she charged past him, threading the gap between the reversing truck and the service entrance.

"What the fuck!" "Crazy bitch." She heard this behind her, but who cared, because now she was past the work site, on open sidewalk, and there was a bank window sufficiently mirrored to give her a view of herself. She lifted her shirt high, nearly to her bra, provoking an appreciative whistle from the workman she'd rushed past. In the gray-tinted reflection, the scar didn't look inflamed or split or anything. And now the stinging had stopped.

She sank down, wiping fresh sweat off her forehead. She took out her phone and called Dr. Robeson's office right there, and listened to the nurse's soft prerecorded voice tell her the clinic's business hours and then give an emergency number. She dialed that number. It rang four times and then the line clicked and disconnected. She stared at her phone, trying to think. Her back no longer hurt. Her legs still felt full of ice water, but her back? It was suddenly as if nothing had happened.

21

Not a word from Samantha as Catherine came in late. She didn't even lift her gaze off her monitor. Catherine let out a showy sigh before crossing the office, past other cubicles and the fogged, empty water cooler. She sat down into her desk's gray glow and monitor sizzle, feeling light sensitive, feeling weirdly permeable.

"Everyone's heard about Baltimore, yes?" Samantha called out across the room. She was standing at her desk. "So if anyone feels even *remotely* under the weather, you can't be here."

The other girls kept their attention on their own terminals. Only one glanced over: the underfed-looking Korean girl wearing the sleeveless McGill sweatshirt, an ink stamp from some nightclub like a bruise on the back of her hand. "Are you okay?" she whispered. Catherine knew her name: Theresa; Samantha had barked it across the office once. Theresa was one of the girls who'd been promoted to phone work. Catherine smiled and nodded. The whooshing sound in the ceiling vents changed pitch. An office chair squeaked. Catherine's MR server windows tiled open, the top three requests flagged red for urgent.

If their lunch breaks coincided, Catherine thought, she'd follow Theresa out to the street and introduce herself. Usually she sat on a bench in Greeley Square, ate a sandwich, and watched the cabs lock, listened to the horns go. A conversation, she thought, a little human contact with someone other than Frances and Laird, would be good for her.

Catherine tiled forward a few MRs and forced herself to clear them. A weeklong standing appointment with the Russian-speaking reflexologist at the Four Seasons Toronto, a new game console for a member's twelve-year-old son's birthday, a Swiss-made air purification system for a Montana ranch.

Not today. She couldn't do this today. It took practically zero concentration, but she was drifty, thinking about too many things. She reached around and again ran her fingers along the scar. Maintaining this perfect posture was starting to hurt. She tentatively sagged into the chair back. And felt—nothing. She decided it had been a pinched nerve, or a muscle spasm, and that she'd overreacted. She pulled her left arm and then her right across her chest, rolling her neck to ease the tension there.

The room was dead still, just creaking chairs and hushed telephone voices and cooled air moving around.

She tiled forward the next MR in her queue and *finally* there was a phone number in the instruction field. Coded R for restaurant, D for discreet.

She clicked open the member's bio. Alex Hamburg, executive at Lazard. Upper East Side address. Married. Wife's birthday six months ago. Daughter, Louise, at Lawrenceville, turning sixteen in May. He was one of the older members. The history file said he was very pleased with the chalet in Courchevel Pursuit found for him, and the birthday gift for his assistant: an antique Tiffany cigarette case.

She slipped her phone headset on—and decided she was losing her mind: twenty-nine years old and grateful for the chance to speak to a restaurant hostess. *No*, she thought, with a satisfying finality. She thought of Frances—the way she'd simply gone to Mercer's office when she was tired of waiting around. Before she could think better of it, she dialed from her keyboard.

Mercer answered immediately, startling her. "Who's this?"

"Catherine."

"Catherine! I was wondering when you were going to call."

"You were? No, you weren't."

"I was on, what are they? Tenterhooks."

"I've left, like, three messages."

"Why are you whispering? You're calling from your desk?"

"Yes, it's—" Catherine started. Samantha was out of her seat; the girls in her immediate vicinity were trying to listen. "Can I talk to you about something? Maybe I can come there."

"What's Samantha doing right now?"

"She's—" Catherine checked. "Coming over. Can I?"

"I've got someone here."

"Oh—"

"Aha," he said quickly. "Ha—I know how that sounded. I've got Fritz. You remember Fritz. Down from upstate. Gracing us with his presence."

Samantha was standing beside Catherine's desk, waiting, apparently, for her to finish. Catherine kept her eyes on her screen.

"Improvements to the HideAway," Mercer said. "Then, expansion. Franchising. Keep it under your hat. But we're almost done. Are we almost done, Fritz?"

Fritz spoke in the background, barely audible: "You talk too much."

"So you want to come down here?"

"Affirmative."

"This is an emergency?"

"Not exactly," Catherine said.

"Come whenever."

Catherine flipped off the headset and stared up into looming Samantha—all four foot, eleven inches of her. "It was Mercer," she said.

Samantha gestured that Catherine should stand, and when

Catherine did, she pointed at her bag, which Catherine duly scooped up. Turned out Samantha could really motor on her doll-like legs, and Catherine had to jog after her down the hallway, past the cacti, the sagging bookcases. Samantha opened the door of one of the small, cramped offices and nearly pushed her in. The freebies lay in heaped piles: poly-bagged cashmere sweaters, snorkel masks in plastic cases, tennis rackets with tags leashed to their strings.

Samantha was tense, intent, and Catherine shrunk from her. "You book the hotel rooms," she said. "The airplane tickets. You do what you were hired to do."

Catherine waited.

"What did you call him about?"

"Just a . . . I had a medical question."

"He knocked you up. You need an abortion."

Catherine laughed without meaning to. "No. What?"

"You're not sleeping with him?"

"Not at all."

"You're too old. I saw that the first day you came in here, which means I should have turned you around and sent you home. If Mercer is fucking you then you're a known quantity. But if he's not fucking you, then I don't know what your purpose is."

Catherine had no idea what to say to that.

"He finds me staff. He finds clients. All fine. But then he starts, what"—she dropped her voice—"shooting people? For money?" Samantha took another step into Catherine's space. "Our operating reserve is down to zilch, we might not make payroll next week, and I've got half our members asking me to put them on the waiting list for this place—I have no idea what this place is."

"The HideAway," Catherine said.

"I don't *want* to know. What I want is for you to book the hotel rooms. The airplane tickets . . ." She trailed off. Shook her head.

"I only went once, a month ago," Catherine said.

"Open your shirt."

"I'm sorry?"

Samantha mimed unbuttoning and spreading her shirt wide.

"I don't think so."

"Let me speak into the microphone then," Samantha said, leaning into Catherine's chest. "There is a line between what I do and what Mercer does. I put up money two years ago, and so I run this place. But I have spoken to a lawyer about that and ten thousand dollars does not make me an accomplice to whatever the fuck."

"You think I'm wearing a, what, a wire?"

Samantha waited, simply staring at Catherine's chest. Catherine thought, *Okay*, and unbuttoned her shirt.

Samantha used both hands to hold it open, looking hard at her bra. She let the shirt go. "Why are you calling Mercer?"

"Mercer's our boss. Your boss."

"Because he has you reporting on me?"

"To whom?"

"You tell me."

Well, this was an absurd conversation. Catherine started buttoning up. Before she could stop herself she asked a question: "Do you know Dr. Robeson? Sandy Robeson?"

"Who? Why would I?"

"You're Mercer's business partner."

Samantha took off her glasses and rubbed her eyes. "He tried to tell me about hiring that maniac from Scotland and I threatened to quit. He told me about bribing some helicopter pilot and I threatened to quit. He told me about some miracle TX cure, and I threatened to quit. There's the legitimate piece to this business, and there's whatever Mercer's doing, and you're calling him for some reason, and so you have to go."

Catherine thought of the binder clip Samantha had shot at her. "You're not the easiest person to work for."

"Has anyone been killed?"

Catherine let out a surprised hiccup of a laugh.

Samantha fished among the shopping bags and came up with a black one: Cartier. "Here," she said, handing it over without checking to see what was inside. "A parting gift."

22

Sprung into Manhattan's vertical sunlight, Catherine scooted away from the construction site, feeling only the reflected heat off the limestone to her right, feeling nothing that could be called emotion. What just happened? Had she been fired? Inside the Cartier bag was a bottle of perfume. She didn't want it. She set the bag on the sidewalk and continued toward Fifth Avenue.

A billboard displayed giant models breathing through the lifted hems of skimpy T-shirts, staring dolefully at the intersection. No motto, just the brand name—ENDLESS SUMMER—in overlarge capitals slapped across the image.

Had she lost her health care? Her paycheck? The answers would start to sink in any minute.

She heard a noise behind her, a couple of shrill screams, and had to leap out of the way of a young man in torn jeans barreling his way down the sidewalk. He had dreadlocks and wore a dingy T-shirt that read, in inked letters, I AM THE SUPERBUG. Four or five soiled cotton masks were slung like kerchiefs around his neck. He smiled at Catherine and then coughed on her. She felt the light spatter on her chin and smothered her face with her sleeve.

He coughed in Catherine's direction twice more. She shrank from his open mouth and gray teeth.

He jogged ahead. He coughed on two women, who yelped and scattered. A cab waiting at the red light sounded its horn; the driver's head and waving arm popped out of the open window. Another pedestrian took two loping steps and executed a short, piston-like punch to the back of the man's neck. His head snapped forward.

Furiously wiping her face, Catherine picked past a heap of trash bags and retreated into the shaded entry of an office building. She stood there taking short shallow breaths. *I'm okay*, she thought. She dug in her bag for her antiseptic gel.

There was commotion out on the street, shouted voices, more honking, and then, suddenly, gunfire. She felt it before she heard it, a thumping on her chest, like a doctor hitting her with a mallet. She covered her head and crouched. Looking up, she scanned the stopped traffic, people running this way and that. Then she saw them: police with their weapons crossing the intersection. Catherine dropped all the way to her stomach as they fired dozens of rounds. The plate glass of a bank spiderwebbed. She peeked up from the sidewalk and the young man was lying flat. There was a liplike wound in the crown of his head.

The energy around Catherine shifted to panic. In a moment, she heard the sirens and started running with everyone else. She made it a block before she noticed a car keeping pace with her, silent on its electric motor. The window went down and out came music that was solid hollering, drums like firewood dropped down a chute.

Chad pulled his sunglasses off and lowered the volume barely at all. "Get in," he said.

23

Chad sped along the bus lane, bullying through traffic, sideswiping a man holding a deli bag. The bag went flying. Catherine whipped her head around, horrified, but they were moving too fast and the noise assaulting her from the car's speakers meant she couldn't hear anything. The no-frills dashboard had a heater knob, many blank panes of plastic. She pressed the radio's power button and the thundering music quit.

Her eyes widened at a bus bumper racing up at them. Chad smoothly steered around it, threading an impossibly narrow space. "Can you slow down?"

"Not yet." The knuckles on his punching hand were beet purple. He gripped the wheel like a Formula 1 driver.

Catherine couldn't catch her breath. She closed her eyes, saw the man's open scalp, the pooling blood—and popped them open.

Chad zigzagged through the Garment District, running four red lights. "There," he said, easing off the gas as they zoomed past the Flatiron Building. "We should be clear."

Catherine finally got her breathing under control. "You *hit* someone." She worked her death grip off of the armrest and craned her neck over her shoulder.

"Had to get ten blocks out. They'll overreact, cordon the area. They always do. That guy got you, didn't he?" At a red light Chad turned to look. She shook her head, not liking the clinical way he was studying her. "Yes, he did. But you're okay." Chad rubbed his eyes, put the sunglasses on, and loosened his tie. They were on Fifth Avenue, approaching Mercer's block.

"Did he say we were friends in college?"

"Who?"

"We weren't. He didn't give guys like me the time of day." Chad pulled beside a fire hydrant. "Plus his GPA wasn't that good. He's sort of an idiot."

Chad cut the engine. "Catherine Mayville, he says, like I should know your name. But turns out you're Catherine *Duval*. If I'd known who your father was I never would have agreed."

Catherine took a moment to respond. "To what?"

"You read the NDA?"

She hesitated, then nodded.

"Tell your dad about Cytofit and you'll disappear. He'll disappear." The door locks clicked open.

"It's a hydrant," was all she could think to say.

There was pure condescension in Chad's expression.

24

Mercer looked delighted to see them. "Hey, stranger," he said to Chad. His shirt was open at the neck; he wore wrinkled suit pants and a pair of loafers. A cheap pen nestled behind his ear. "How did this happen?" he asked, pointing at the two of them.

"She was up on Thirty-Third. *Working.*"

"Sure," Mercer said. "She pitches in from time to time."

"She had a little incident with a propagator."

"A *what*?"

"Some anarchist kid looking for attention. DOH cops took him out. Like they're supposed to."

Mercer landed a hand on Catherine's arm. "Are you okay?" She registered his light touch, the reassurance meant by it.

"Can I use your bathroom?" Catherine asked dully.

"Know where it is?"

She nodded. Sunlight sat hazily on the dusty length of the conference table. Newspapers, stapled spreadsheets, and a laptop computer were piled together at one end. Around the barrier, Mercer's office carried a thick smell of dried sweat, coffee, and menthol soap. His large canvas satchel erupted with shirts and boxer shorts; a twisted sheet and pillow lay across the daybed. She wanted to stretch out and close her eyes and try to forget what had just happened. Instead she went into the bathroom, where shaving cream and a razor lay beside the sink, a hand towel draped over its edge. She ran the water and scrubbed her face and her hands with antibacterial wash. She found a fresher towel on a hanging rail and buried her face in it for a long time.

"I've been trying to reach you," she heard Mercer say.

Catherine came around the folding screen. Chad was casually bouncing billiard balls off the bumpers. "Life's busy," he said.

"I sent a proposal over to your office," Mercer said, bent over the conference table, making orderly stacks of papers. "Bet you haven't had time to read it."

Chad flung a ball hard into the corner pocket. "Your driver around? I could use a little of his pick-me-up."

"Let me call him." Mercer scooped up his phone, sweeping his thumb across the screen. "Want me to call Frances too? Make this a party?"

"How about a trip upstate?"

"The HideAway's already got a four-month waiting list. Word of mouth is beyond belief. Laird and I have been taking guys up twice a week."

Chad pursed his lips. "Pursuit members?" he asked.

"A flood of them. And we're attracting bigger crowds too. Still just using fifties but the other night there must have been a hundred locals ready and willing. Times are hard I guess."

Chad flung another ball against the bumper. "You know who her dad is? Obviously not."

Mercer turned to Catherine.

"What's my dad got to do with anything?" she asked.

"Tell him," Chad said. "How many million did he get?"

"He gave it all away," Catherine said automatically. It's what she always told people when her dad's story came up—for the folly of it, not because she was so proud.

She quickly explained the Pfizer case to Mercer, said it was ancient history, which it was—thirty-five years ago—but when she was done he tipped his head and blew air up at the ceiling. "How did I not know about this?"

"Because you're not *careful,*" Chad said. "An heiress, a socialite, a big name," he added, doing a fair imitation of Mercer's voice.

"It's all true," Mercer said to him.

Catherine, bewildered, stared into the space between them. "No it's not."

"She's your *employee,*" Chad said.

"And I'm lucky to have her," Mercer said lightly, flashing the barest look of warning at Catherine.

"Her dad tried to take down a pharmaceutical company."

"Just makes it better." He smiled. "Duval and Mayville. I can't believe how perfect. The press will be all over her."

Chad pulled balls out of the side pocket. "I did read your proposal."

Mercer clapped his hands together. "Compelling pitch, no?"

"No."

"How did you feel up there blasting away? Weak? Afraid? No, you didn't. The opposite of afraid. You felt powerful. *Invulnerable.*" Mercer circled to the heap of pages on the table. "You've seen these new studies on viral susceptibility? It's all mental. You're depressed, anxious, fearful, whatever, you're—what is it?—forty percent more likely to catch TX. Fifty percent? I've got the report somewhere." He made a show of shuffling through some papers. "The HideAway isn't just fun with guns. It's about staying *healthy.* I know we've got some security issues, and we need better site control. We should lay down a chopper pad in a secure spot behind the motel. But that's just funding. That's just a million. Two, two point five. A rounding error to an outfit like yours."

Chad let out a dry laugh.

"Pocket change. Come on. You'll get an equity stake."

"Obviously," Chad said.

"Look at these revenue models," Mercer said, kneeling on one of the strung-cable chairs and pointing at some spreadsheets on the table. He unfolded a huge road map. Two areas were circled in red. "The numbers hinge on expansion, on getting sites we can control. Fritz has some leads." He pointed at both circles on the map. "An old gun club north of Poughkeepsie. Then there's an abandoned summer camp just over the border here in Jersey."

"Fritz is a felon."

"Some white-collar thing a decade ago."

"He's bribing the police."

"What do you care? Remember: one point two million median annual salary, slightly under half married, most have higher degrees, barely any children. They're up at the HideAway every Thursday and Saturday night. They're exactly who Acetor wants. You need me to get to them," Mercer said. His gesture included Catherine. "You need us."

"I don't *need* you for anything."

A burr of irritation made it into Mercer's voice. "Did I steal your lunch money in college? I'm sorry. Okay? Don't let some childish shit get in the way of seeing the potential here."

"I barely remember you from college."

"Well, that's not true," Catherine blurted. "You should have heard him in the car. He needs us for what?"

"Take me up," Chad said.

"And you'll think about it," Mercer said.

"Take me up tonight," Chad said. He took a breath and spoke more quietly. "Clear the schedule."

Mercer scratched his scalp thoughtfully. "Can't."

"Fine. Fuck you and your proposal." Chad started toward the door, pointing at Catherine as he passed her. "Remember what I said."

"It's just—" Mercer chewed on his top lip. "There was a sort of unfortunate incident last night. Kid lost an eye."

"What?" Catherine asked.

Mercer nodded gravely. "Fritz spreads the word about goggles, but ..." He spread his hands helplessly. "Anyway, tensions are running a bit high. This kid was popular in town."

Chad stood by the entry.

"All I'm saying is it could escalate pretty easily. Lotta hunters up there. Good ol' boys with guns."

Chad cleared his throat and let a thumb-sized wad of phlegm drop into a cactus plant.

"Piss in it. Cacti are indestructible," Mercer said.

Chad put his hand on the door. "Call when you have the helicopter ready," he said.

25

Words rushed out of Catherine: "He threatened me. Threatened my dad."

"I can't get over that about your dad," Mercer said, trying to refold the road map.

"'You'll disappear. He'll disappear.'"

He flapped the map open, tried to fold it again. "Chad's all bark."

"But he's the reason I have this?" She pointed at her back.

"I'm the reason," Mercer said crisply.

"Okay, but he's the one *threatening* me."

Mercer stepped around the table, closing the distance between them, sliding his hands into his pockets. "Everything's fine. Better than, actually. We're going upstate tonight, Chad's on the hook. Sure: Cytofit's sensitive. Chad wants a controlled rollout. So you really can't talk about it."

He was looking at her with total focus, the way he had up at the HideAway. She thought of that thick, enveloping smell in his office and caught herself taking a deep breath, trying to draw a vestige of it in.

"A kid lost an eye?"

"That was for Chad's benefit. His inner Rambo." He laughed. "Keep up, Cate."

"With what? *You haven't told me anything.*"

Mercer hopped up on the conference table, hands under his legs, feet crossed at the ankles. "That's because I'm under a pretty heavy NDA too. But look, okay . . ." He lowered his voice, as if there was anyone near to listen in. "I get this call in February. Chad says his name and then nothing, as if I should know who he is. Well, turns out I should. I went to Princeton with the guy: Chad Bonafleur from the Nursery Fund—which is like a . . . a coven. You go in with a couple million and suddenly you're Bill Gates. No one knows how he does it. Crazy gains every month and it's just him—no partners, no assistant. Chad basically can't work with people, and god knows whose money he has. When I get the call I figure he's got a new girlfriend who needs a pair of shoes or a table at Masa. I'm like: ten-thousand-dollar initiation, blah blah, doing my Pursuit pitch."

"Why are you whispering?" Catherine asked.

"He wants to talk about some company called Acetor, staffed with boy geniuses from MIT working on a TX killer. Holy grail, he says. Immunity. But there's a problem, which he can't tell me about until I sign what has to be the most threatening NDA I've ever seen. The problem is Acetor's market research: Americans will take a pill, nose swab, even a shot. What they aren't up for is something under the skin. The boy geniuses tell him they've done market surveys and the word 'implant' has negatives through the roof. So I ask him, why are you telling me? His answer: Because *you* can change that. You can turn Cytofit into a must-have. You first, then your Pursuit people." Mercer paused, his shoulders hunched. "I have barely a second to work that out. All I can think to say is, *I'm* not the guy. But I can get the right person for you."

Catherine stared at him.

"Then I met you. And I thought, *Perfect*. An heiress. Intelligent. You've been at the right parties. You've stayed off the gossip pages. You're gorgeous and confident. And all of that was right in his face at the HideAway. Chad's just too much of an asshole to say so."

This was more flattery, but Mercer sounded sincere.

"You and I didn't 'meet,'" Catherine said. "You called me about a job. Out of the blue."

Mercer hesitated, squinting his eyes, thinking. "Someone mentioned you to me. I think. I was looking for another client handler and your name came up."

"Richard Tramway recommended me?"

He shrugged.

"But you didn't *tell* me about Cytofit."

"I couldn't because of the NDA. I figured if you didn't want the thing you'd just say no. But why would you? Who wouldn't want to be immune?"

"*You* didn't."

"No—I'm *dying* to get it. I'm just not pretty enough to be the first."

She thought of that stinging tremor in her back. "So I'm the only one who has this," Catherine said.

"For now," Mercer said, slipping off the table, closing the distance between them. "Give us time."

"You say that like I'm involved. How did Chad know where I was today?"

"Right time, right place. Or maybe he's *following* you." Mercer placed his hands on her hips and backed her to the polished concrete wall.

Catherine tensed.

He lowered his head to hers and kissed her high on the cheekbone. She smelled his minty soap and thought of the twist of sheet on his daybed.

"No, no—don't." She put her hands on his chest and pushed gently. "The thing that happened." He kissed her neck. She admitted that this felt good, even as she wondered if she should stop him. He buried his fingers in her hair.

"What about Frances?" she said, thinking of the sounds she'd heard rising up through her floor.

"What about her?" he asked.

"Come on." She pushed him, more firmly this time. "You're together."

"Hardly. I'm here all the time."

"I've heard you."

"You heard *Laird*—the two of them. I'm not kidding. He told me."

And then Mercer's hands were under her shirt and her blood was up and she was giving in to it. He sank to his knees and kissed her bare stomach. She thought of the propagator dead in the street. She thought of the man Chad had sideswiped with his car, saw his deli bag sailing through the air. She thought of herself with a gun snug on her shoulder, taking aim at a crowded stretch of road. Mercer found her pants button, her zipper.

26

"I'm pretty sure Samantha fired me," Catherine said, half-wrapped in a sheet, flat on the daybed, dizzy, a tingling net of sensation on her skin. Amazed at what had just happened.

Propped on one elbow, Mercer traced a figure eight around her breasts and gave her an amused grin. "Fine. You're well out of there." He sat up, his long back glinting with sweat.

"But I need the money," she said.

"Soon as Chad's on board, I'll cut you a check." He hooked his boxer shorts over his narrow hips as he examined something on his laptop screen. "Till then you're living rent-free, right? Life is good."

She blushed. "I did ask if that was okay. You never called me back."

"It's fine," he said, and smiled. "Do me a favor? Call Laird and tell him to phone the pilot."

"So—we're done here?"

He kissed her lightly, then again, on her ear, sending goose bumps down her legs. "Lots to do. Big night ahead of us. Gotta contact Fritz, make sure he can get ready in time."

She saw herself as she had been moments ago, on top of him, her feet tucked under his legs, and then felt a tightness in her throat. Hungry—that was all it was; she was always hungry after sex. She used to make Phillip get out of bed, get dressed, and venture down to Seventh Avenue to pick up a slice of pizza for her. Total sweetheart: he always had.

Typical that she thought of Phillip after what had just happened. After Mercer had gotten her off so expertly.

"You're up for it, aren't you? The HideAway."

"I'm invited?" Catherine said, sitting up, holding the sheet to her, glancing around for her underwear, the embarrassing, threadbare white cotton ones she'd tossed away before Mercer could get a good look at them.

"Frances too," he said, and slipped into the bathroom. "Call her for me?" She heard him turn the water on.

She dropped the sheet, stood in the middle of the office, wearing only her socks, feeling more exposed by the second. Finally, she spotted her underwear, clinging to the rim of the trash can.

27

Catherine hurried down Broadway, scrolling through her phone for Frances's number, raking her hair flat. Mercer had almost dismissed her there at the end. And yet? Her wrists ached pleasantly where he'd pinned them to the daybed. The high sun felt warm on her face. She listened to songbirds on a light post, a sound like giggling. The fact was she'd enjoyed herself, every moment of that—it surprised her how much. A viscous globule of bird shit went *splat* on the sidewalk not three feet in front of her and she almost laughed.

She'd left while he was showering, but there was a part of her that wished she'd stayed. Forced him to the daybed for another round.

Only Chad threatened her mood. She wished she'd stuck up for herself. She wished she'd told him she didn't like rich assholes who thought they ran things. *Tell your dad about Cytofit and you'll disappear.* Actually that's exactly what she *should* do. She wouldn't say she had it. Just pick his brain. He might have heard something about an immunity implant. If he went on a crazy rant, she'd just hang up on him. She'd done it before.

So she skipped over Frances's number and dialed her father instead. Five rings, six rings. A woman's voice answered.

"Hello?"

"Who's this?" Catherine asked, startled.

"Um, who's this?"

"I'm Jack's daughter."

"Oh! Hi . . ." The woman stretched out the word. "This is Deborah. Your father's . . . Well, let me— Let me get him for you."

Yellow police tape marked the northern boundary of Union Square. She rarely came this close to the park. It had been a temporary holding zone, and like the far West Side, the streets around it had never recovered. Now it had this homeless encampment you could smell for blocks. She could see the nylon tents and overturned shopping carts between the sycamore trees. The smell of smoke was thick; some kind of bonfire had been set just beyond the pavilion. DOH officers stood in small clusters along Seventeenth Street, a few of them speaking into their radios. She turned on Park.

"Catherine," her father said, his tone doubtful. "What a surprise. I— Risotto's almost on the table, so can I call you—"

"Risotto?"

"Lunch."

"Oh, okay. It's just your only daughter, Catherine. Whom you haven't spoken to in—"

He interrupted her: "I called and called. You never called me back." This was true. The job, the move—she'd simply stored his messages, telling herself she'd return them later.

"You're right. I'm sorry, Dad. I've been busy. Do you have a minute?"

"Are you okay?"

"Who's Deborah?"

Her father just cleared his throat.

"Is she your girlfriend?" This seemed impossible.

"She's not my girlfriend," he said.

She headed east on Nineteenth into the cool shade of a pair of ancient city oaks. Sturdy green trash cans lined in plastic stood at all four corners of the intersection.

"It worried me, not hearing from you."

But he didn't sound worried. He sounded distracted, like he wanted off the phone. "Some changes," Catherine said. "New job, apartment." More silence on the other end of the line. Had he heard what she'd said?

"Hang on, duck." The sound was muffled—he must have cupped the phone—but Catherine could still hear him say something like, "Keep it warm? I'll be off in a sec." He cleared his throat again. "Sorry about this. It's . . . we're about to eat."

"Risotto. You said." Catherine tried to imagine the kitchen fragrant with cooking, a woman moving around the gas burners. She didn't want to let him off the phone. "Who is she?"

"Deborah? She's just . . . she looks after me. Duck, I can't really talk right now."

She held her breath for a moment, stepped into the alcove of an apartment building, and spoke into a cupped hand. "Dad, have you heard of something called Cytofit?"

"Say again?"

"It goes in your back and protects you from TX? Do you know what I'm talking about?"

Five seconds passed. "Deb, sorry, I need a minute. I know. I'm sorry. This won't take long. Let me just switch phones. Keep it warm." When her father came back on the line, his voice had changed. He was gruff, commanding: "Say that again."

"It's supposed to make a person immune," she said.

She heard his breath.

"You can't tell anyone I'm asking."

"It's in you now?"

"I didn't say that."

"Who makes it? What doctor gave it to you?" he asked.

Catherine was silent.

"What *doctor*?" he hissed. "Give me his name."

"Never mind."

"How'd he talk you into it?"

The cell phone was hot on Catherine's ear. "I was just *asking*."

"Come home," her dad said quietly. "Go to Penn, get on a train. I'll pay for the ticket."

Come home. How many times had she heard him say that to her mother over the phone? She remembered spying on him from the second-floor landing: her tall, handsome, broad-shouldered father staring gloomily at the front door, as if willing it to open and his wife to walk through.

"I'm not taking a train home," she said.

"You're in trouble."

She'd come out of the alcove and was walking fast, nearing the Department of Health personnel station on Third Avenue. A small demonstration was in progress beside the main entrance. HEALTH CONTROL = MIND CONTROL read the cheap signs carried by a circle of men. Why was it always men? Men her dad's age: gray, balding, unshaven, chanting themselves hoarse. They followed each other in a tight circle. Tourists took pictures with their phones.

"I shouldn't have called," she said—and she meant it. "I really shouldn't have called." Cabs were streaming by. She realized where she'd been headed, toward this run of elegant Gramercy dwellings, a limestone town house with brick coping and a paneled door.

"Don't hang up—"

"Enjoy the risotto," she said, and pressed the phone's red button. Simultaneously she jammed her other thumb on the Acetor clinic buzzer, flush in a strip of brushed aluminum beside the door. She rang and rang, rubbing her eyes with the bony part of her wrist. Why was she crying?

She backed up nearly to the street, craning her neck. Through the windows she could just make out the black leather cushion of the sofa in the waiting room and the slick leaf of a potted palm. She thought of Robeson's face. She'd trusted him because he was handsome.

You're in trouble. No, she wasn't. And she didn't need her father to look after her. Idiotic to have called him. Idiotic to be crying about it.

She'd ruined her good mood. Falling into bed with Mercer had cheered her like nothing had in weeks. She wished she was still there.

She walked south and west, toward Soho. She dialed Frances, dully reported the news: "Mercer says we're going up tonight."

"About time," Frances said.

Catherine heard another voice behind Frances's. "Is that Laird? He's supposed to—"

"I'm waxing his chest," Frances said. "For better muscle definition. Also helps with his pain threshold, which between you and me is not very high. Just ripping a—" Catherine heard Laird yelp in the background. "There," Frances said.

"Chad's coming too. And Laird's supposed to call the pilot."

"Were you with Mercer?"

"I wasn't. I'm running an errand."

"What errand?"

"Frances, forget it."

She could hear Frances and Laird talking. Frances came back on the line. "He says we shouldn't go. Says some kid got shot—" Her voice moved away from the phone. "Why are you such a pussy? Listen—he screams like a girl. Ready?"

Laird yelped again and Catherine ended the call.

28

April would approve, Catherine thought, sliding around in the Audi's backseat. April Mayville would approve of the recklessness of heading up to the HideAway less than twenty-four hours after a local boy—a football player at the nearby high school—had had his cornea perforated by plastic pellets fired by a grossly overpaid corporate lawyer, age twenty-seven, a Pursuit member who hadn't been sorry, who had said, according to Laird, "Get the kid a fucking Band-Aid and reload me." She'd have approved of the way Catherine overcame her alarm that this really *had* happened with a single bump of coke, snorted off Laird's tattooed knuckle. She would have approved of Catherine's not bothering to do up her seat belt on the drive to Mercer's office. She would have maybe raised a glass to the idea of not doing up seat belts in general. She never wore hers, had been unbuckled the night she'd driven into a tree.

"This," Laird said, idling at a red light, "is a terrible fooking idea."

"It'll be fine," Mercer said. "Stop scaring the girls."

"Plus the pilot's soused."

"He's what?" Frances asked.

"Reached him at the bar," Laird said. "Supposed to be the man's night off."

"Chad's excited is what counts," Mercer said.

"Fook Chad," Laird said.

"Do your big theory," Catherine said, leaning forward, teasing Mercer, geared up on the coke.

"Cate," Mercer said.

"Shooting people makes you Superman," she said. "Makes you *healthy*." Catherine sat back and caught Mercer's careful, attentive gaze in the side mirror. She smiled. "Expansion, right? Two and a half million? Do the speech you did for Chad."

"Ms. Suddenly I Know Everything About Everything," Frances said.

Laird turned, looked at Frances, mock-punched her knee. "That nutter better not take aim at you again."

"Or you'll what?" Frances said, a grin emerging in her sullen expression.

"Look at you," Laird said. "Christ, you're gorgeous."

Frances raked her hair out for him and kicked her feet up between the front seats, showing off her legs as if he was the most popular boy in school.

29

Chad was already at the heliport when they arrived. "Not them," he said, pointing at Catherine and Frances. He'd ditched his suit coat and tie, rolled his sleeves up over thick forearms.

"Why not? Break up the testosterone," Mercer said.

The pilot was standing nearby, his feet wide apart as if trying to hold his balance, clicking a pair of mints against his teeth. Chad tapped his nose at Laird. Laird pulled the plastic envelope out of a pocket. "Attaboy," Chad said, taking it from him and throwing a feint with the other hand.

Laird ducked backward and then said, "Steady."

Chad smiled and dug into the coke with his car key, snorted up a heaping mound, and tossed his head up like a pony. "Spin around for me," he said to Frances.

"No way, perv."

Chad liked that. He handed the baggie sideways to Catherine, then pulled it back when she reached for it, like bait on a line.

"He told me you're good at parties."

"I'm terrible at parties," Catherine said.

He laughed and tossed her the coke. "Bring them," he said to Mercer. "Whatever you want."

The pilot declared to everyone in earshot that the helicopter was fueled and ready. What did Catherine know about helicopters? Still, she thought it looked better than last time: shinier, the soot marks near the tail rotor scrubbed off and the cabin aglow with captured sunlight. She keyed up her own helping of coke and moved away from Chad.

The drug made her head effervescent, soda water ear to ear.

"Nice day for flying," the pilot said.

And it was a nice day, a clear and pleasant summer afternoon, which made it all the more unsettling when they lurched sideways gaining altitude and then swiveled as if blown by a gale. Laird stripped off his headphones and shouted over the roar. "Told you he's fooking soused."

The helicopter steadied. The streets of Jersey City, as they swung over, were striped in shadow.

30

There was no one at the landing site, no one in either direction on the two-lane road. Once the thumping of the rotors quit, the rural quiet was interrupted only by the calls of birds and the early evening breeze bothering the branches.

Chad turned to Mercer. "A hundred guys you said."

Where were the police? Where were the sawhorses blocking traffic? A collection of orange cones lay scattered around, capsized from the wind shear.

"So, we're early," Mercer said. "It's fine."

The sun dipped the rest of the way below the trees and bands of colored light reached across the sky.

The pilot spoke over his shoulder, into the cabin. "I can't leave her without police."

Mercer popped open the cabin door. Cool air rushed in. Up the paved path, at the entrance to the HideAway, Fritz stood backlit, waving them inside.

Laird, Frances, and Chad stepped out of the helicopter. The pilot said it again: "Can't leave her here without—" He took off his sunglasses, rubbed his bloodshot eyes, and flipped a bank of console switches with the side of his hand. "Jesus."

Fritz shouted something at them. As Catherine hopped down to the road, she made out the words. "*Inside,*" he was saying. "Get *inside.*"

At that moment, a yellow pickup truck rolled into view. It stopped a hundred yards away and both doors opened. A big man in a sweatshirt and a NASCAR hat and a teenager in what looked like a camouflage-print jumpsuit emerged. The big man lifted his phone to his ear and spoke into it, but he was too far away to be heard.

"Let's go, folks," Mercer said, and gestured up the path.

Catherine followed Laird and Frances. Mercer and Chad trailed her, walking backward, staring down the length of the road. "I told you not to come," Fritz said when the group reached them. "I said to let things quiet down, but here you are."

The man and the teenager stayed put, leaning on the hood of the truck, staring at them. The man pocketed his phone.

"It's the boy's father and brother," Fritz explained, and typed something into a keypad, cutting the lights in the airlock. "Shame about the boy. He was set to start as running back next season."

"Fritz goes to all the local games," Mercer said.

The room was unchanged from a month ago—wagon-wheel chandelier, mismatched rugs—except it was stuffy with a thick chemical smell, and a new pair of foxes had joined the collection of taxidermy, baring their teeth at Catherine from the bar. The light from the table lamps was muted, atmospheric, cut only by the flickering colors of news on the TV. No volume, so Catherine couldn't hear the commentary, but the banner at the bottom of the screen read: BIOTERRORISM IN MIDTOWN. She crossed to one of the leather chairs and put her hands on it. The reporter stood in front of a cordoned stretch of Fifth Avenue, then the picture cut to aerial footage of the intersection with Thirty-Third, crowded with DOH vehicles and men in biohazard suits.

"There goes our ride," Frances said. She'd split the gingham curtains and was peering out one of the windows. Catherine heard the turning of the helicopter blades. Frances called over to Mercer: "Okay, genius—how do we get home?"

Chad joined Catherine in front of the TV for a moment. "I told you they'd overreact."

"Seriously," Frances said. "I'm not spending the *night* here."

Chad left Catherine and swung open the door of a glass case holding the riot guns—four of them, racked upright, fat barrels and grooved plastic stocks lit by hidden bulbs—and snapped two out of their cradles. He tucked boxes of shells under his arm and started toward the ladder and the roof hatch.

"Who are you going to shoot, mate?" Laird asked.

Mercer smoothed his hand across Catherine's back, pressing her toward the ladder. "Don't worry," he whispered.

She wanted out of this room and its dank, chemical stink. So she followed Mercer to the ladder and trailed him and Chad up it, taking the rungs in twos, climbing toward the open hatch and fresh air.

31

Laird and Frances sat on the lounge chairs. Catherine remained on her feet and tried to appreciate the soft, warm evening, the aroma of pinesap from the nearby branches in her sore nostrils. She'd just done another bump of Laird's coke.

Chad bent over the rail, leaning out, aiming one of the riot guns at the empty road, searching for something to shoot at. Finally he fired—a throaty popping sound. He worked the pump and fired again, aiming at the truck.

"It's too far," Fritz said.

"It's moving," Mercer said. And he was right. From where Catherine stood she could just see it: the yellow pickup coasting slowly down the road, engine silent, headlights off. Chad tracked it with his gun, obviously pleased, his body easing into its stance.

"Still too far," Mercer said, looking through binoculars. He swept them in the other direction, then back again.

Chad fired, kicking up dust in the road ahead of the truck.

"Are we even using this thing?" Frances asked, releasing her ears, pointing at the rubber slingshot coiled on the decking.

Chad dug in his trouser pocket. He tossed her his money clip. "I've got some fifties."

Frances waited a beat before pushing herself off the lounge chair. She collected the thick billfold. "You sure do."

The truck rolled closer. Chad traded the gun for the other he'd brought. Sliding four shells into the magazine, he kicked the discarded weapon toward Catherine. "Load her for me."

Catherine didn't. She kept her eyes on the truck. Chad shot and she heard the tinny clatter of pellets against the front hood.

It stopped. The driver's-side door opened and the teenager spilled out onto the road, stumbling as he hit the pavement. Tucking something into his body, he ran hard for the trees. Mercer moved along the rail, watching him. Chad fired three times. "Little fucker's fast," he said.

Fritz's face was tense. "We should go downstairs."

"Give me a turn," Frances said, standing and reaching for the gun that lay on the deck. Catherine watched the passenger door of the truck open and something long and narrow slide through the gap. There was a coin-sized glint of reflected light.

She didn't see Mercer lunge at her, wasn't prepared to be brought down so hard on her belly. The air went out of her chest as a sharp report echoed across the bowl of the sky.

Frances was down too. She and Laird lay in a heap at the foot of the lounge chairs. And Fritz had his palms flat beside his chest as if stuck at the bottom of a push-up.

Another shot went hissing over their heads. Catherine pressed her face into Mercer's arm.

Chad knelt, methodically reloading, no hint of panic about him.

"You're okay," Mercer said, gently untangling himself from Catherine, drawing his arm out from under her forehead, and crawled over to Chad. "Get away from the rail," he said.

"Is that a fucking rifle?" Chad said, leaning closer. He sounded excited.

Another shot kept Catherine flat on the deck. It nicked the steel rail with a blue flash. Frances squirmed under the lounge chair, her hands pressed to her ears.

"We're fine," Mercer said. "The angle is too steep."

Fritz, in a crouch, shook his head. He pointed. "The boy's climbing a tree on the far side."

Chad steadied his gun's barrel on the railing, gripping it one-handed, holding his head and body back. He fired from that position, the gun leaping with the recoil.

Another rifle shot cracked and ripped through the branches above them, bringing down torn leaves like confetti.

"Fook me," Laird said. He picked up the second gun and shoved in shells from one of the ammo boxes. He crouch-crawled to the opposite end of the platform. Just beyond his head fireflies drew curlicues in the dim light. In the distance, in the notch cut by the road, the horizon was a hyphen of red.

The next rifle shot was lower, a waspy whine louder than the rest, and Frances yelped again. Both Chad and Laird fired twice in response and the clamor put Catherine inside a bell. Chad drew the box of ammo closer to him.

Fritz aimed the binoculars across the road, into the woods. "The big oak. One o'clock. You see him?" he asked Chad, rolling the focus. "About ten feet up in the branches."

"Which tree?" Laird asked.

"Your three o'clock," Fritz said.

"Wee fook, fifteen feet up?"

"Get below," Mercer said to Catherine.

But Catherine was already on her way. She'd spent the last few seconds coaxing Frances from under the lounge chair and dragging her along the catwalk toward the hatch. The girl moved stiffly, the corner of her lower lip stippled with blood.

32

Catherine poured vodka over ice and drank it quickly, her hands shaking. She dug a fingernail into the grain of the wooden bar. The gunfire upstairs—audible despite the closed hatch—was a mocking, brutish vibration inside her skull.

"Take it easy, C," Frances said. "Don't have a *stroke*." Once they'd gotten downstairs Frances had undergone a quick transformation, shaking off her panic, appearing—suddenly—calm. She settled on the bearskin rug, blotting the blood from her lip with a paper towel.

"*You*," Catherine said, "were white. I had to drag you down the ladder."

"Yeah, thanks," Frances said, rolling her eyes, then gazing wistfully up at the ceiling. "Now we're missing it."

"Missing what?"

"It's a setup. I bet you a million dollars. Fritz hires two locals to shoot blanks or whatever. Chad gets his rocks off. Mercer waves the white flag and everyone goes home. Chad is so excited he writes a big thank-you check." She let the paper towel drop. The bleeding had stopped.

"Those were real bullets," Catherine said.

"So the guys are aiming to miss. It's like"—Frances waved her hands—"serving nonalcoholic beer at a party. Stupid girls think they're drunk." She pointed upward with the bloody paper towel. They listened to Chad whooping between shots.

Catherine remembered Mercer tackling her, his body landing on hers, the shelf of his rib cage jarring into her. "He would have warned us."

"*Mercer?* Are you kidding?"

The hatch opened; both Catherine and Frances flinched at the leap in volume. Laird dropped out of the racket, pulling the hatch closed behind him and nimbly skipping ladder rungs on the way down. He hit the floor with both feet, waggled a finger in his ear, and jawed his mouth open. "Fritz says he has a pair of shotguns, real ones, in a room down this way." He pointed farther down the corridor.

"Tell her," Frances said, standing and spreading Chad's cash and credit cards on the bar.

"Tell her what?"

"It's a game, or a prank or whatever." She picked through a pile of bills. "Mercer set it up. Those are blanks."

"Blanks? Fook no. Bastards go by like hornets," Laird said, and then disappeared down the hall.

"Check this out," Frances said, holding a plain white rectangle embedded with a silver microchip. She tipped it back and forth in the light. A DOH ID—Catherine recognized it immediately. Officers flashed them at pedestrians before doing breath checks. The agency's holographic shield threw off a prism of light and color.

"Put it back," Catherine said.

Laird returned holding two shotguns that even Catherine could tell were real. They had heavy wooden stocks—not plastic—and leaner, longer profiles. "Ammo's below there," he said.

Concern rippled across Frances's placid expression.

"Fooking weird setup he's got," Laird said, rummaging around. "Surveillance monitors and such. Pour me a bit of that vodka, Cathy?"

Catherine slopped an inch into a fresh glass. Laird toasted her and gulped it down, his Adam's apple working. "Up I go," he said.

Frances's eyes were wide, her nonchalance gone. "Seriously, Laird," she said in a strained voice Catherine had never heard her use before. "Stay."

33

Minutes passed. Catherine wasn't sure how long. She and Frances jumped at each successive round of gunfire, and then what sounded like a cry of pain from the road. They heard Chad let out a celebratory whoop.

Frances raced to the big window. Catherine approached the smaller one and cautiously tipped the gingham curtain. The view wasn't great. Too much shrubbery on the HideAway's slope. Still, she could just see the truck, which was shot to pieces. The windshield was shattered, the hood pockmarked, the tires flat on their rims. A man lay beneath the passenger door on a bed of sparkling glass.

"That guy is *so* not moving," Frances said.

"Nailed that motherfucker, didn't I?" This was Chad descending awkwardly from the hatch. Catherine's breath caught: he was splashed in blood, his dress shirt soaked with it, his left arm hanging limp at his side.

"You're shot," Frances said.

"Grazed," Mercer said from the open hatch. He started down the ladder as well.

"Worse than that, mate," Laird said, coming down too. "Oi, Chazza. Pressure to the wound."

The blood ran thickly down Chad's left arm. He looped his gaze drunkenly around and spotted his cash, cards, and money clip on the bar. He scooped them up, leaving a smear of blood, then turned his drained face on Frances.

"Oh, gross," Frances said, staring at the blood dripping off his cupped hand.

"Come here," he said to her.

"Let's clean that up first," Fritz said. He was the last down the ladder. He took the medical kit down from the shelf, separated out gauze, tape, and a pair of scissors.

"*First?*" Frances asked. She turned to Mercer. "Get him away from me."

Mercer was tense. "Sit down, Chad. Let Fritz sew you up."

"Oh, *nice*," Frances said backing up against the fireplace, her voice rising. "Nice. You're worried about him."

A violent, sudden motion. Chad took Frances by the throat, forced her down to her knees.

Frances let out a strangled cry, her eyes bulging. She swung her fists wildly, and one of them connected high on Chad's arm, near his ragged, puckering wound. Dark, plummy blood dripped freely down his left side. He grunted and let her go, tottering on his feet.

Laird shoved Chad away. Chad stumbled and slipped in the mess he'd made on the floor. He then gave himself a slow, sleepy appraisal, shoes to shoulder. He performed a single, woozy blink.

Catherine had gone to Frances, to help her to her feet. "Are you all right?"

Frances shook her off, braced herself against the wall, holding her throat, staring fixedly at Chad.

At that moment, a faint thud and crack was heard from the roof.

They all looked up—all except Frances, who came at Chad, the side of her fist moving in a wide arc. The girl was half Chad's weight, but she connected, right below his chin. He staggered back again. "Don't fucking touch me," she said.

"Fritz," Mercer said. "Keep him conscious."

The sweet smell of gasoline threaded into the room. Tendrils of acrid smoke ghosted along the ceiling. Nose in the air, Fritz took himself swiftly to the ladder.

Catherine turned to the window and spotted a pair of teenagers on the slope. One, wearing a sleeveless Knicks jersey, lit a handkerchief stuffed in a beer bottle. He lobbed it impressively, high and out of sight, a sky hook in the direction of the roof. Behind them, in the road, stood a half dozen men—all of them with rifles—one of whom was speaking into a megaphone. The only words Catherine made out were *come out* and *surrounded*. Another man stood in the bed of a newer, bigger truck truck—not the one Chad had shot up. He had his rifle at his shoulder, aimed in her direction. There was a single, muffled crack. Inches from Catherine's face, the glass jellyfished, and her head flew back.

34

What a relief to be walked, a hand on her wrist, through the smoke. What a relief to keep her burning eyes shut, to blindly put one foot in front of the other, to follow where others led (a kind of perfection, she realized, of her life up to this point). The roof was on fire. She'd been shot in the face. She kept seeing the glass whiten; she kept seeing the bloom of fissures. Had the window held? Or had tiny shards blown into her eyes?

The hand was Laird's. Or she thought so. She put one foot in front of the other, eyes closed, and listened to the pings and thuds of bullets hitting the motel, a sound like hail.

She tasted smoke in the air. Laird turned her through a doorway—"Step up, step up," he said, then ordered her to sit, then seated her, fairly hard in fact. Down she went on her butt; she fell into a cool stone wall.

"Ouch," she said.

"She speaks," Frances said.

"Are my eyes—" She touched her cheeks, terrified to feel a horror of blood and goo.

"Bulletproof glass, Cathy," Laird said. "Look at me."

Carefully, she did.

"There's a girl."

"It's like the comatose club around here," Frances said, and indicated Chad, slumped against the opposite wall. Beside him stood a worktable arrayed with glowing screens; beside Catherine there was an army cot scattered with taxidermy catalogs and German-language newspapers; in the corner, a sink and open shelves stocked with canned vegetables and soups. She took it all in, a back-and-forth view. She could see! Her eyes were fine. They burned and teared—but that was just the smoke. A thin layer of it floated in the room.

Catherine felt the back of her head. A huge lump, tender to the touch. That must be why she felt so cloudy, so leaden. "I fell down?"

"Did you fook," Laird said.

"I hope he bleeds to death," Frances said, wiping her own tearing eyes, massaging her throat. She sat on Fritz's cot and nodded at Chad, whose eyes were closed, his mouth slack.

"No, you don't," Mercer said, leaning over Chad, stuffing gauze high on his arm, looping it with a length of bandage.

Fritz typed a code into a keyboard on the worktable and vents high on the wall turned on. The hanging smoke stirred and started to dissipate. Another combination of keystrokes brought a line of surveillance feeds onto the screens. They gave views of all points around the motel, but every screen was bad news. Men with guns, smoke and flames, dead static.

"This room is protected, vapor sealed," Fritz said, almost merrily. "They can burn the whole place down around us, and we'll be fine right here."

"They are burning the whole place down," Laird said.

"Define 'fine,'" Frances said, staring at the metal toilet half-concealed by a cotton curtain. The room was tiny, and already feeling uncomfortably warm.

"Fritz? Little help?" Mercer asked, sitting on his haunches.

Fritz looked critically at what Mercer had done, the bandages uncoiling on Chad's arm, the blood still flowing out, and then at Chad's chalky face. He crouched down and rewound the bandage, cinching it tight.

"Ow," Chad said sleepily.

"Hey, you," Mercer said. "Stay with us, buddy. Let's get your phone out." Chad didn't respond, so Mercer began rooting in his trouser pockets. "Password, Chad," he said, finding the phone. He lightly smacked Chad in the face. "I need your phone's password."

But Chad's head was drooping under its own weight. "Who . . . are you calling?" he managed.

Fritz frowned at his equipment. One by one the screens were cascading into static.

"The cavalry," Mercer said.

35

They watched the helicopters circle in on the one functioning surveillance feed. The grainy, smoke-clouded image showed two of them hovering, sweeping the road with floodlights. They watched ropes uncoiling, men with automatic weapons zipping to the ground.

"Do you know how . . . expensive this is?" Chad croaked out.

At a thud on the steel door, Fritz broke the vacuum seal, slid it open, and a pair of uniformed medics wearing respirators came in out of the billowing smoke. They assembled a folding stretcher beside Chad and escorted them through what was left of the Hide-Away. The lobby was now a smoldering ruin: acrid smoke, blackened walls and leather chairs, the bulletproof windows punched out of their frames.

Catherine took deep breaths of fresh air when she got clear, then slipped and fell on bullet casings scattered on the wet grass. The teenager with the Knicks jersey lay only a few feet away, the grass saturated and sticky with his blood. A uniformed officer approached with a sheet of black plastic, the radio on his shoulder squalling. More bodies lay on the road, already covered in plastic. *Six*, she counted, and felt the wet earth through her jeans.

Chad was carried past her on a stretcher and loaded into one of the helicopters, which immediately lifted and banked away. Two armed men remained, as well as a pair of officers speaking into radios, standing near the second helicopter.

She tried not to stare at the plastic heaps on the road. One of the armed men, linebacker-sized, lifted her up from her sitting position and hauled her down the path, automatic weapon bonging at his chest. He herded her together with Laird, Frances, and Mercer. They were ordered to produce their MED cards, which they did, like chastened schoolkids. All except Laird. "Not a US citizen, mate," he said.

"This one's a minor," the other officer said, busily scanning the cards one by one. He spoke quietly into a microphone on his shoulder: "Scottish national, male, and female minor, last name—" He read it off the scanner screen. "Wrightman. W-R-I . . . First name, Frances. Greenwich, Connecticut. Here's the address." He read it aloud too. "Yep. Got that?"

Frances's expression was stricken. "They're *not* taking me there," she said to Mercer, who ignored her. Catherine kept her eyes rooted to her boots, which were caked in ash and mud.

They were ordered into the helicopter, a bigger, more utilitarian cabin than the one they'd flown here in. Frances sat across from her, her fingers clasped in Laird's. The men, DOH shields embossed on their helmets, remained on the road as the rotors started to turn, stirring the smoke in the air. No one spoke. Frances's face was streaked with soot and sweat. Catherine's mind was an empty room. This was shock, she thought as they lifted off, and she tried, and mostly failed, to see anything through the high window, but then they banked and she got a view through scrims of rising smoke and ash of the firing platform on top of the motel—now a blackened pile of lumber—and one last view of the bodies lying in the road.

RICHMOND

36

"Six men killed in our little adventure," Catherine said from her slumped position on the sofa. Almost seven on a Tuesday evening and she was still wearing the pajama bottoms and thin ribbed tank she'd woken up in. She hadn't left the apartment all day, hadn't showered since yesterday morning, and could smell a stale odor under her moisturizer cream.

Mercer dropped his bag to the floor and kneeled at her feet. He'd just come in. "Lost any sleep over that?" he asked, and ran his hands up her legs. Her pajama bottoms had a white ribbon tie, which he tugged loose.

In fact she saw the bodies every night on the ceiling of her room, getting smaller and smaller as the helicopter carried her away. But not because she was plumbing her conscience; it wasn't as if she thought *she* had killed those men. What Catherine was doing was simpler, helpless: returning again and again to the rough charge of that night. She saw herself wired on coke. She felt the impact on the wooden deck as the first rifle shot hissed overhead. She saw Chad, covered in blood, take Frances by the throat; she watched the bullet burrow into glass just inches from her face. She saw commandos sliding down ropes, flashes from their gun muzzles lighting surveillance screens.

"Not one news story about what happened?" Catherine asked, her pulse quickening. Mercer was tracing invisible lines up her inner thigh, through the thin cotton of her pajamas. "How are we not all over the Internet?" It seemed incredible to her. "How do they do that?"

"Kidding me? They do that all the time."

They being the DOH. Sometimes she told herself this was why she was still sleeping with Mercer: because sex was when he explained things. The money Chad's fund managed was government money; the Nursery's purpose was to find small private companies and start-ups for the Department of Health to invest in. The sort of discreet investing the CIA had been doing for decades. "I guessed early," he told her, proudly, in bed. "That car he drives is DOH-issue. And the way he acts? Like no one can touch him? He's a violent guy behind a desk. That night turned him on in a big way. His whole definition of a good time has changed."

"He almost bled to death."

"Which, you know, you're not to tell anyone."

"Who would I tell?"

Mercer seemed so pleased with himself, so *happy* about how things had gone, that Catherine began to think he'd planned everything. "*Did* you pay those guys?"

He just laughed. "You're flattering me." In fact, he said, he'd had to think on his feet, gambling that he could pull a DOH number off of Chad's phone, gambling that whoever answered wouldn't want anything to happen to their star investment guru.

There'd been a massive transfer of funds into the Pursuit bank account, presumably to pay for a new HideAway. Mercer wouldn't say how much, but he had immediately written Catherine a check for $20,000, which more than cleared her credit card debt. Her share of her mother's inheritance was finally out of probate too. Catherine was suddenly the richest she'd ever been.

The money connected in her head, in an electric way, to the bodies covered in plastic, to the smell of gasoline and the taste of smoke. To the sessions with Mercer when he pushed her against the mattress, when she took him by the hair and pulled hard enough to leave strands of it between her fingers. Sometimes she told herself she was fucking him for information; most of the time she knew the truth: that she was doing it because she liked it.

Catherine stripped her musty tank top off and felt the sofa's cool leather against her back, felt it everywhere but the numb seam around her implant scar. She bent forward, tasting the dried sweat on Mercer's neck—a faint white line of it under his jaw. Mercer slid his own hand between her legs, pressure that made her catch her breath. She lifted her hips and slid her pajamas off.

37

When Mercer wasn't around, there was no one to talk to. Nothing to do. The DOH had deported Laird to Scotland and delivered Frances to her parents' house in Greenwich. A shame, Mercer said. They were fun to have around—but honestly? It was easier not having to keep their mouths shut about Cytofit.

He was constantly rehearsing his marketing plan: the Pursuit members who liked the HideAway would *love* the invincibility that came from having a virus killer in their backs. They wouldn't care about FDA approval, which was years away—or they wouldn't once they met Catherine, he said. As soon as Chad gave the go-ahead, they'd throw a few parties to tell them about Cytofit. She'd say there were no side effects and get the guys to sign the necessary releases, just as she had. "We make it screamingly expensive. We starve the demand. We give the *Times* an exclusive," Mercer said. *We, we, we.*

In the meantime, have fun, he said. Catch a movie. Go shopping. She tried that. She ducked into a few stark, gallery-like spaces, ignoring the coolly appraising salesgirls, her mind going quiet at the trim stacks of shirts, the airy racks of dresses, the single bag on a lighted shelf. Then, on the corner of Spring and West Broadway, she saw the man in the Yankees cap, the one she'd spotted in Herald Square. Broad shoulders, sunglasses, stubble on his jaw. He stared steadily at her. She turned around and quickly walked the block, making three rights. He kept pace.

"Probably," Mercer said when she asked if she was being followed. His own new driver was DOH. "They're keeping tabs on me too."

"They who?"

"DOH. Whatever. Chad's people."

Chad was still recovering from his wounds, Mercer said. That's why he wasn't returning texts or calls. But Mercer wasn't wasting time. He had found one hundred acres for sale in remote western New Jersey. He was getting bids from contractors for the new Hide-Away.

To celebrate he hosted a happy hour at his office. The sheer novelty of being around other people got Catherine there, in a print minidress and heels. She downed a couple of glasses of tequila to loosen up and watched Mercer order the caterers to lay everything out and then leave. "I'll call you when it's time to clean up," he told them. "You look good," he said to her.

"Thanks," she said, picking a strand of hair off of his blazer sleeve.

The men started filtering in at seven. She remembered sitting in her cubicle, wondering if she'd ever meet these guys: dark suits, fat Windsor knots, bright pocket squares, heavy steel watches, more or less the same short haircut. Young, most of them. Late twenties. Thirties. Mercer kept her close, clapping each guest on the shoulder, calling him by name, and introducing her as Catherine Mayville. They ate tiny croque monsieurs and poured themselves scotch and laughed at each other's jokes. Some of them were friendly, some wanted to know if Mayville meant *that* Mayville, and all of them, every last one, assessed her body as if she were a prize heifer.

Mercer smiled at the attention she was getting, and by the end of her third drink she found she enjoyed it too. She contentedly listened to them debate the merits of Chinese energy companies, compare English to Italian shoemakers, or agree that the back nine at Torrey Pines was a real fucking bitch.

When the room was full, Mercer stood on a chair and tinged a glass with a spoon. He apologized that the HideAway had been out of commission. "Maintenance issues," was how he put it. "No big deal." The good news is he'd found a new site and was already breaking ground. "This new place is going to be incredible. Bigger. Completely secure."

"You been up?" asked the guy Catherine was standing next to— olive skin, yellow shirt, horn-rim glasses, class ring from Yale.

She nodded.

"Fun, huh?"

"Depends what you're into."

"You're his girlfriend?"

"Definitely not."

He laughed and nodded, like Catherine had told some terrific joke.

"They ate you up," Mercer said after the party, back at the loft. "I knew they would." They climbed the stairs to her bedroom, hers as usual, because his room was three deep with cacti.

"I was the only girl in the room."

He pulled her dress over her head before they were through her door. She turned to kiss him, a little drunk still. He pushed her backward onto the unmade bed. He kneeled between her legs and put his mouth on her, briefly, teasing her.

She took handfuls of sheet, closed her eyes, and let herself go. He was good at this, took his time. But not tonight: Mercer roughly flipped her onto her stomach. "Condom," she said, surprised and breathless. Feeling his erection on the back of her thigh.

They'd always used one, even that first round in the office, but this time he made no move for the bedside drawer. Instead Mercer reached up along her neck and crushed her head into the pillows. She turned her face to get some air. "Wait," she said. He was hurting her.

She tried to prop herself up and he put a hand between her shoulder blades, pinning her with it. He forced his way inside her and she gasped. She reached and buried her fingernails into his hand. "Stop it," she said. "*Stop.*" Catherine threw her elbow into his chest, connected squarely, and heard him exhale in surprise. He trapped her arms. She fought off a rush of panic, tried to keep breathing, tried to say as clearly as she could: "Mercer, *stop* it. *Now.* Stop."

He didn't, not right away. He shoved deep inside her and then sighed, released her arms, and pulled himself out. She practically leaped off the bed, a hot flush across her face.

"I can't feel anything with one of those on," he said simply, as if nothing had happened, and kicked the top sheet to the floor.

"What the fuck?" She spat the words at him. "You're confused about 'stop'?"

"Aren't you on the pill?"

"Like *that's* the issue." She crossed the room and stood in front of the bathroom mirror. She took in the sight of her washed-out skin. "You've slept with how many girls? Just in the past year?"

"None," he said. "You."

She laughed.

"You don't believe me."

"I told you to *stop.*"

Mercer rubbed his face with his hands, stood up, and joined her in the bathroom. Behind her he palmed her ass, then slid his hand up to the implant scar. "Thought you'd be into it. You were. Before," Mercer said, kissing her on the ear, dropping his hand to her breast. "I'm sorry."

"No, you're not." She pulled away from him, slid a towel off the rack, and wrapped herself in it.

Look at me, she thought. Minutes ago she'd wanted his hands on her. Now she wanted to be as far away from him as possible. She turned on the water and shied back from the freezing spray.

38

"You should hear the way he talks about that night," Catherine said. "Like he's proud of it. Like there was this grand plan."

"I thought you said there was," Krupa said. "You said he wanted—"

"Not them burning the place down. Not having to call in the DOH. Mercer just thought he'd show Chad a good time and get him to invest."

"You're losing me. Chad is who again?"

"Runs a hedge fund." And then Catherine dropped her voice beneath the Velvet Underground—"Sister Ray" turned up loud enough to mask the fact that the restaurant was half-empty. "Works for the DOH."

Krupa turned her phone over on the bar next to her Campari soda, which she'd barely touched. She crossed her mantis legs and regarded Catherine coolly.

"He finds stuff for the DOH to invest in," Catherine explained quietly. She checked to make sure the bartender wasn't listening in. "Research they want to support but keep private. Now he's investing in Pursuit." Catherine took a furtive sip of Patrón. She checked herself in the bar's smoked mirror. *God* it felt good to spill a few of her secrets. Tell Krupa more. That's why she'd texted her for this drink.

"Shooting people for money is the thing?" Krupa asked, eyebrows up. This was the part that interested her.

"Plastic bullets," Catherine repeated. "No one's supposed to get hurt."

"It all sounds a little . . . fucked up," Krupa said.

Catherine nodded. *Tell her about the bodies. Get it out of your system. Tell her you've been followed.*

Tell Krupa about Cytofit.

She was boiling over with talk—compulsively, because it felt so good to unburden herself about the HideAway. But she was boring and alarming Krupa—she could see the reactions on her pretty face. It hadn't escaped Catherine's notice how amazing she looked, with her flawless cocoa skin, her hair cut short. She wore a loose T-shirt with no bra, pencil skirt, and heels. Catherine had done her best, a nice pair of jeans, ballet flats, Prada top, but she knew she appeared pale and a little haunted by comparison. The solitude had been getting to her. Since the party, since that night with Mercer, she'd been anesthetizing herself with talk shows and Frances's months-old fashion magazines. Forgetting to eat, to change her clothes, to shower. A suspended midair feeling, each day a marathon to get through. Catherine felt the sting of the cuts she'd made with the kitchen knife.

Tell her about that. *The worst thing.*

The strange, discomfiting pulse had returned. She'd felt it a few times, deep in her back, when she switched on the microwave or got close to the TV. Like a live wire kicking around deep in her muscle tissue. Painful, but only for a second. She hadn't told Mercer because he kept going on and on about what a miracle Cyto was. And if it wasn't? If there was something wrong with it?

The other night after he'd gone to sleep she'd felt the sting hard, reared up in bed, and ventured down to the kitchen. She boiled water in the kettle and poured it over a chef's knife. She stood naked in front of the hallway mirror, a damp washcloth in her mouth, and tried to aim the heated blade, getting mixed up, moving it left when she wanted right. Pressing the edge of the blade against the scar tissue felt *wrong*, funny-bone wrong.

She pushed harder, drew a line of blood, and the scalding pain made her bite down on the cloth between her teeth. She let the blade hang. Felt the blood trickle down her back. She turned and stared at herself in the mirror. What was she doing? It was like snapping out of a trance. She was going to *cut it out herself?*

Tell Krupa. That she was losing it. If she didn't the drink was going to end and she was going to have to go back to that vacant echoing loft.

Krupa glanced past her and shook her head. "God, this place is *dead.* Have you been to that new hotel on Vestry?"

Catherine shook her head.

"It's got this amazing basement—like three stories underground. They have a stage for bands and I mean the strongest fucking cocktails."

"I haven't been anywhere."

"Well, you have to know this guy, and you have to go super late, like four. But I'm sure I can text you his number."

"Get another," Catherine said. "There's something else."

Krupa smiled. "Dinner plans. And actually, I sort of should—"

Catherine blurted: "I think . . . I might be in trouble."

Krupa waited a beat and then settled on her bar seat and re-arranged her legs and smoothed her skirt. "Mercer Kerrigan," she said. "I mean, I've seen him around but isn't he a bit, I don't know. Beneath you?"

Yes, an old part of her responded.

"Phillip was so lovely. And you two were a great couple."

"Can I show you something?" Catherine was already reaching behind her, underneath her shirt, and peeling the tape away from the bandage she'd put on this morning. The bar was empty enough, and dim enough, that she could show her without drawing too much attention.

Krupa lifted her hands as if to protect herself from whatever it was.

At that moment Catherine's phone buzzed. A text message from Mercer lit the screen.

Coming to pick you up.

Catherine let the hem of her shirt drop.

Krupa had read the message too. Catherine turned the phone over on the bar and darted looks around her. A few couples at tables. The bartender. Two young guys at the end. No one she'd seen before.

"Hey, listen," Krupa said, startled by the expression on Catherine's face. "It's Lorraine at dinner and some other girls. You could totally . . ." She trailed off.

She hadn't told Mercer she was meeting Krupa. There was no way he should know where she was. She'd been careful walking over here. Checking behind her. Doubling back.

"I'll text you the address," Krupa said. She folded her hands on top of each other on her lap, seemingly unsure what else to say.

Breathing was like trying to pull air through a sheet. Catherine forced herself to smile.

Krupa squeezed her leg. "I'm worried about you, C."

Catherine was worried too. They air-kissed good-bye—inches of space between their faces.

39

Outside it was a summer night, the stink of garbage in the gutters. Catherine walked away from the restaurant, heading south along Sixth Avenue. She wasn't being followed. She kept turning around to check. She passed a hissing neon sign in a streetwear boutique and had to grit her teeth against the spasm beneath her skin. An ice-water tingling traveled up and down her legs.

She should power down her phone. Drop her MED card into the gutter. It's what her father would tell her to do. She thought of him, thought of their last phone conversation. Weeks ago he'd known she was in trouble. *Come home*, he'd said. *Go to Penn, get on a train*. It didn't seem so absurd to her now. Maybe he could help her. She had the money. She could buy a ticket. To Richmond. Anywhere.

The West Fourth subway was three more blocks. She could see the station's lit-green globe above the parked cars. *Run*, she thought. But it was barely the start of a plan. And the sound of a car's horn to her immediate left wiped it clean out of her head.

Mercer was in the backseat, his phone lighting his hard face. He spoke to her through the open window. "You tell her anything?"

"I can't go out and get a drink with a friend?" she asked.

"Don't be dumb," he said. "You know what you can and can't do." The front window powered down and the driver behind the wheel—slicked-back hair, thick neck, fingerless gloves—gave her a steady, professional gaze. "Get in," he said.

Catherine stayed put. People passed on either side of her, and she wondered how she looked to them—how unsure of herself, how in need of help.

Mercer rubbed his eyes with both hands and blew out a long weary breath. "Oh, I'm having a fucked-up night. How about you?" he asked the driver. "You having a fucked-up night?"

The driver's eyes didn't move off of Catherine.

"Marcello? Antonio? Giuseppe?" Mercer shrugged. "Won't even tell me his name. Won't talk to me at all. Like he's mute. I didn't think it was possible to miss Laird so much." Mercer reached over and opened the passenger door from the inside. "I'd do what he says."

But still she stood there. "How did you know?"

"Chad called me. Described the person you were with. Wanted to know her name."

Catherine absorbed that.

"So I need to know what you told her."

"That I was seeing you. That I haven't hung out with anyone for weeks. That I'm bored out of my mind."

The driver cursed under his breath and started to open his door.

"*Okay*, okay," Catherine said, lifting her hands. Reluctantly, regretfully—she let herself in.

Mercer put his hand on her leg.

"Don't," was all she said.

She took a deep breath to control herself. "'Chad's all bark.' Remember that?"

Mercer said nothing for seconds. "Maybe it's good news. This command appearance. The geniuses at Acetor finally ready to do some fucking business."

But Catherine saw how edgy he was, how nervous—and she

pressed herself into the seat, really ironed herself against the leather.
They weren't moving fast. She could still run. She could pull the
door handle, tumble out, and probably not hurt herself too badly.
They crossed Lafayette, Mulberry, Elizabeth. At every intersection,
she debated; she slotted her hand into the car's cutaway door lever.
Her best chance was at Chrystie; the Grand Street station was *right
there*. But the driver's eyes met hers again in the rearview mirror and
the leveled threat there told her to wait.

They turned onto Essex; the housing towers above them were
dead dark. This was the far corner of the Lower East Side. You didn't
come down here anymore if you could help it. As if to prove why, a
man came swiftly toward the car at a red light—soot-black hollows
under his eyes, a set of stained teeth. Seeing him, the driver opened
the glove compartment and pulled out a nickel-plated handgun with
a squat piggyback attachment riding the barrel. The man had some
kind of tool—a hammer—in his hand. He raised it to smash the Audi's window. The driver threw the door into him, knocking him down.
Then he stepped out with the gun.

Catherine knew she'd screamed only from the scoured feeling
at the back of her throat. Her ears rang from the shot; the man's
body slapped to the asphalt. Mercer's head rose up from between
his knees. The driver spoke into his phone. He kicked the body out
of the way.

"It's okay," Mercer said. "They use tranquilizer studs. Giuseppe
there phones it in and a van picks the guy up. He'll be in Newark
before breakfast. Poor bastard."

"Quarantine?" Catherine whispered. The man lay sprawled, no
visible blood.

Mercer shrugged. "That's just where they send people."

40

They parked beside Chad's light-blue compact at a five-story stone building blackened with soot. The windows were narrow and dark, the glass gridded by wire, and a faded sign advertising Yung Foo Reflexology hung above the door.

They were under the Manhattan Bridge, not far from the river, nor from the homeless camp beneath the FDR. Catherine could make out cardboard-and-aluminum shanties—as well as the moonlit twinkle of the water. Also down there was an Astroturf park where a group of men, all wearing masks, performed Tai Chi exercises under street lamps.

Mercer's phone chirped; he didn't bother to answer it. "Wave at the cameras."

She kept her arms at her sides and instead examined the very clean, very vigilant-seeming derelict camped on the building's stoop. Beneath a stained blanket and scattered newspapers, she spotted his holstered gun, fitted, she noticed, with the same bulbous attachment their driver's had. A bullet-shaped thermos stood nearby, open and steaming. He looked them both over and then nodded at the dark scanner panel beside the building's steel door.

"It's retinal," the man said. "Just stare into it."

Mercer climbed the stoop and leaned forward. A green light pulsed in the lower corner of the panel. Catherine was next. Up close she saw her own eyeball as a dark planet hanging in the glass.

The thing in her back twitched as the scanner sent its waves out over her. The green light pulsed again.

"You jumped just then," Mercer said.

Catherine didn't respond. The door's lock clicked. The derelict drank from his thermos.

41

They rode the elevator to a floor with acres of beige carpet, striped by protective plastic. In the shadows several rows of workstations stood empty. Just beyond them Chad's office ran the width of the building. His dark shape moved in the frosted glass, like a fish in a murky aquarium.

Mercer led Catherine past the workstations, knocked, and slid the office's panel open. "This is a hell of a place to get to," he said.

Chad set his phone down, banked flat-panel monitors on his desk lighting his wide face. He didn't look good, dressed in a T-shirt, his right arm bulked up by bandages, his eyes drugged and glassy.

"You know we were almost carjacked?" Mercer asked.

"Close the door," Chad said.

Mercer did so uneasily. A pair of windows to her right gave a view of the street and the heavy stonework of the Manhattan Bridge. Another set of windows behind Chad framed the span of the river and the floating lights of Brooklyn. A calming distance— she wished she was on the other side. She wanted to put miles between herself and this room.

"Sort of inhospitable, not having any place to sit," Mercer said, looking around the bare space: a pair of filing cabinets, a dying ficus plant, nothing else.

"You won't be here long," Chad said. He spoke to Catherine without looking at her: "Who were you with?"

She resisted the urge to check with Mercer before answering. "A friend."

"Name?"

"Just an old friend of hers," Mercer said. "Krupa. I know her."

"Krupa what?"

"Chad—relax. Two girls having a drink."

But he looked relaxed, that was the thing. His eyelids were weighted. His body utterly still. He tapped something on a keyboard.

"Can we talk shop, maybe? Like the rollout? Where are we?"

"Delayed," Chad said without looking up.

"For how long?"

"Hard to say."

Catherine thought simply, *Of course.* But Mercer's expression turned angry. "What's going on?"

"They're reevaluating their marketing plan," Chad said. "They want to go in a different direction."

"*You* decide what direction they go in. You're the one with the—"

"They polled the words 'implant,' 'antivirus,' and 'Department of Health,'" Chad said. "The results were not good."

"They *polled?*"

"Anonymously. A third-party survey. Public resistance is insurmountably high."

Mercer looked stunned. "Your Acetor boys are *clowns.* Any hint of DOH around Cyto and none of my guys will come near it."

"Acetor figures they won't anyway. They're strongly for making it compulsory."

"You called *me*, remember? You knew that if you started with the right people you wouldn't have to go down that road."

"I called you 'cause I couldn't get anyone to tell me where the next Sheetrock gig was," Chad said.

"Bullshit. It was the people I know. The connections I can make for you. They're going to be *clamoring*—"

"It's not the strategy Acetor wants."

"Who cares what they want? Who pays their bills? You do. Come on."

Chad waved his hand dismissively.

Mercer made a sound of disgust high in his throat. "What's changed? You just *funded* me. We're building a new HideAway, re-member? We've got guys lining up—"

"That's off too." Chad stared at his computer screen. He picked up his phone. "Krupa Chatwal," he said into it. He spelled the last name and hung up.

Catherine went cold. Chad sat down with a sigh, swiveled left and right. He flicked something invisible off his desk.

"Chad," Mercer said.

"What did you tell her?" Chad asked Catherine.

"Nothing," she whispered.

"We'll find out."

She opened her mouth to speak, thought better of it, and turned to the window. She had her phone. Call Krupa this second? Before anything happened?

She looked down at the street and watched the driver finish a cigarette, crush the burning end into the hood of the Audi, then open the door and take his gun out of the glove compartment.

"Something's wrong with it," she said. "Isn't there?"

Chad nodded at her, almost courteously.

Mercer was staring at her now. "Wrong with what?"

"You didn't tell him," Chad said.

"Tell me what?" Mercer asked.

"He has no idea, does he?"

"Tell me *what*?" Mercer asked again.

"It hurts," she murmured, relieved to have this out. "It stings and vibrates."

Catherine heard the elevator ding, followed by footsteps. The office door slid open and the driver stepped through, the pistol tucked into his belt.

Behind him, across the empty carpeted space, she saw a lit EXIT sign over a steel fire door.

"It *stings and vibrates*? What the fuck?" Mercer said.

Chad's gesture told the driver to wait. Then he nodded at Catherine. "Take your top off so we can see what you've done to yourself."

"Jesus," Mercer said, starting to laugh, but it was a forced sound. "Everyone calm down."

"With a kitchen knife," Chad told him. And then to the driver: "Give her another minute and then do it for her."

But the driver wasn't giving her a minute. He was coming at her. Stepping out of her shoes, crouching down to pick them up, Catherine thought of all those long days since the HideAway, all the chances to walk out of the door of that apartment. She could have lost the man in the Yankees hat. She could have *tried*.

She had stayed because of Mercer. Sex. Twenty thousand dollars. Loneliness. What an appallingly short list.

42

The tranquilizer stud ricocheted off the door frame as Catherine smashed through. Somehow she kept her bare feet under her down the dim concrete stairs and swung her body around the turn.

She'd thrown her shoes at the driver's face, surprising him. He'd lunged at her—but she'd spun clear. And before he recovered she'd run as hard as she could for the EXIT sign.

Now she heard him curse as she descended another flight, then another, and leaped to the ground floor. She threw her weight into a second fire door and it opened onto a narrow gravel lane at the rear of the building, an eight-foot perimeter fence. No way to climb over—the top was razor wire. But there was a narrow gap at the bottom. She lay facedown on the broken stone and dirt and scooted herself sideways, the spiked ends tearing her top.

Then she was up again and moving, right on Pike Street, sprinting barefoot up the near-empty street, cutting left under the clanking steelworks of the bridge. Keep going or hide? Panting shallowly, she saw blue-white headlights washing along Pike. She crouched in the shadows beside an overflowing Dumpster. The car turned, not the Audi. So Catherine took off again, heading north this time. She tripped on a curb, falling hard on her hands and knees. She scrambled to her feet and turned another corner and then turned the other way, zigzagging, hunting for traffic. She found it on Division Street, stopped lanes of cars, and dashed to the far side, angry drivers blasting

their horns all around her. Across Canal was the subway. Her bare
feet, filthy and black, burned from the rough sidewalk. She was bleeding from both knees. She turned in the warm, doughy air outside a
dim sum restaurant, looking for a place to buy shoes. Behind her a
screaming ambulance stalled in traffic. There: a half block away, Hip
Lee Beauty. Racks of cheap clothes, plastic-wrapped dresses, a wire
display of simple Chinese slippers. Ten dollars each. She ran inside
and grabbed gray ones in her size with a rubber sole and a single strap.
The woman at the register spoke rapidly, hectoring her in Mandarin.
Telling Catherine to get out? Shooing her with the back of her hand.
Still, she took Catherine's money.

Outside, Catherine pulled the shoes on. She collected some
napkins from a bodega and blotted her knees. She powered down
her phone, took her MED card out of her purse, crouched at the
curb, and flipped it into the city sewer. *There*, she thought, walking
quickly away. Just like her dad: *Off the biosurveillance map.* And that
was who she was going to see. *We'll get it out of you.* It didn't seem
the least bit crazy to her now—and she had to trust that he could.

43

She caught an uptown Q train to Thirty-Fourth and walked the single block to Penn Station. It was ten p.m. when she got there, and the departures board told her that the next southbound Northeast Regional didn't leave till midnight. She found an ATM, withdrew six hundred dollars, bought a ticket at the one open ticket window with cash, and then went again to the ATM for another six hundred. She stuffed the twenties and fifties into her pockets.

Catherine settled into a scooped chair in the corner of the waiting lounge, against the wall, with a shrink-wrapped bagel from a deli. She skimmed off most of the cream cheese and then ate it anyway, from the side of a plastic knife. Her knees ached; travelers kept cutting wary looks her way. But none of them were Chad, or Mercer, and that's what counted. She'd gotten away—almost too easily. She wanted to call her dad, but a switched-on phone could let them know where she was. Maybe they knew anyway. She lowered her head, suddenly exhausted, tried to divine her future from the balled-up plastic wrap in her hand.

A layer of sweat dampened her neck. A security guard was marching over to her from his desk. "You bleeding?" he asked, pointing.

She looked at the drops of blood on the floor. Coming from her hurt knee. "I—I fell," she said. "A scratch I guess. Sorry."

"Can't have you bleeding on the floor," he said.

"S-sorry," she said.

"Someone's gotta clean that up. Guess who?"

So she took herself to the women's bathroom, where there were no paper towels, only dented air dryers. She entered a stall and dabbed her raw kneecaps with toilet paper, wincing. Moments later an old woman came in dragging a garbage bag and muttering to herself. She caught Catherine in the scratched mirror. Clumps of her hair were missing. Catherine hurried past her, into the near-empty expanse of Penn. The floor had been polished to a slick gleam. Powerful ceiling vents captured the air. She surveyed the station. The late-night commuters were gone. Now it was just security guards and a small crowd of travelers gathered under the destinations sign, waiting for track assignments. She nestled herself in among them. A woman with a roller suitcase wrinkled her nose and told Catherine to please give her space.

And then finally her track was called; on her way to the platform the sleepy conductor didn't ask for her MED card—he barely looked at her ticket. The seat on the train felt like a featherbed. She flopped into it, reclined, and tried to figure out what she'd say to her dad, how much she'd tell him. Then the train began to move, and she drifted on the shuddering wheels into a deep sleep. She woke to a light-fretted blur of evergreens and placid lengths of bay. The dawn sun was a weak bulb across the Chesapeake.

44

Catherine disembarked in Richmond and gave the taxi driver her old Monument Avenue address. It was early—six thirty—but chances were her dad would be up.

Soon she was passing along the narrow cobbled alley that ran beside her old house, peering through the antique casement window into the breakfast room, seeing not a mess, not piled dishes and strewn food, but a vase of lilies, a clean cooktop, a gently steaming coffeemaker. It was the scent of that Ethiopian coffee that made her homesick. Here was a memory of childhood she actually relished: a girl sticking her nose in the waxed bag of beans and breathing that wonderful, deep soil scent. She made her way to the front door and pressed the bell.

A woman answered the door. She was in her midforties, a round face framed by silver-streaked hair. She wore heavy-rimmed glasses, a University of Alabama sweatshirt, and jeans. She gave Catherine a friendly, sleepy smile. "Can I help you?"

Catherine knew who it was: Deborah. From the phone conversation all those weeks ago. "Is my dad home?"

Still smiling, Deborah took in Catherine's stained silk blouse, her gray slippers. A trace of recognition crossed her face, and the smile guttered out.

45

The shower felt good, her old shower, with its buckling Spanish tile and pounding water pressure. She lowered her head into the spray and replayed her escape from Chad's office. She'd been so good, so quick and nimble, that she allowed herself to hope they weren't looking for her, that they'd simply thrown up their hands and let her go. She saw how naive this was—and yet the feeling grew as she gingerly splashed water across her hurt knees and her scraped-up back, and fended off the shower curtain. She was in her childhood home, she thought. She was safe.

She lathered her hair from a bottle of shampoo that had to be at least fifteen years old—the cheap drugstore brand she'd used in high school. The sweet honeysuckle perfume carried her back. She remembered trying to get her mother's attention, trying to choose an outfit that would be kindly judged by Trisha Heany and Kevan Inglewood at St. Ann's. The names sent a tremor along Catherine's skin.

She shut off the water, wrapped up in the fluffy pink towel, and wiped steam off the mirror on the door. She told herself to go downstairs and apologize to her father for showing up announced. A sincere daughterly apology for hanging up on him all those weeks ago might get that stony look off his face.

Not just stony—he'd looked stunned, then spooked at the sight of her standing in the foyer, as if he'd given her up for dead and yet here she was. He'd bitten his lip; his left hand had given a palsied shake. She hadn't seen him since the funeral. He looked haggard and worn down. His posture was hunched, his eyebrows white and wiry; he'd grown a belly. The weight really surprised her—squash had always kept him trim.

"Aren't you gonna say hi?" Catherine had asked, cutting a look at Deborah. "Your daughter, in the flesh."

He'd pulled her in for a hug. She couldn't remember the last time they'd embraced like that. Not since she was a girl.

"Is everything okay?" she asked him softly. She noticed he was wearing a clean, pressed shirt and new sport sandals on his feet. He smelled of Right Guard.

"You *came*," he said in her ear. "I didn't think you would."

Deborah had been the one who finally spoke: "I bet you could use a shower."

Jack had finally let her go, lumbered past her to the front door; he'd looked out, closed it and threw the latch.

46

Catherine's bedroom was untouched, and in the dresser she found clothes she hadn't worn in years, musty smelling but a good deal cleaner than the outfit she'd come here in. She fished a long-sleeve T-shirt from a drawer and from another, a pair of decade-old jeans, baggy in the way she used to like. Catherine dressed, but before she ventured downstairs, before she made her apologies, she wanted to check something. On the way up the stairs she'd seen that the formal portrait of her mother was missing from its position on the antique console. Where it had always stood there was now a shallow porcelain bowl.

She opened the master bedroom door and peered in. The room smelled stale from a night of sleep, the duvet pulled sloppily up to the pillows. Confirmed: her mother's wedding portrait was gone from the tall Chippendale dresser between the windows, as were April's cut-glass atomizers and velvet jewelry case. Her father's bed-side table was jammed with coffee cups, magazines, and a sloppy stack of printouts from the Web. What her eyes locked on was her mother's table. A tube of hand cream, a half-full glass of water, and a tangle of cheap necklaces.

Catherine closed the bedroom door and headed down the stairs, palming the newel post as she used to when she was a girl. The house definitely had a refreshed, buoyant air. It had been exorcised. She shouldn't begrudge her father a girlfriend. She wouldn't. "Is there any of that coffee left?" she asked brightly, entering the kitchen.

Her father got up and poured her some. He set the mug on the counter and stepped away from it, his attention on the drawn shade of the kitchen window. The coffee was motor-oil black and smelled heavenly. Her dad tipped the shade with his finger, peering out toward the street.

"Jack," Deborah said. "Leave it."

He went to his chair and sat stiffly on the edge of it, staring down into a small china dish and his glass of tap water. The dish held three small circular pills. Catherine spoke directly to her father. "I'm sorry, Dad. I really should have called—"

"It's in her," he said. "It's in her and she wants it out."

Deborah rubbed his back. "She's here to see her father," she said. "She's fine. Everybody is fine. Isn't that right?"

Catherine locked eyes with her father.

"You must know they're tracking you," Jack said.

"I don't think they are," Catherine said into the silence, trying to sound confident. "I got rid of my MED card."

"*Obviously* they are."

Deborah directed a pained smile across the table. "Catherine, listen. Your father doesn't handle surprises well."

"Don't patronize me," Jack said.

"I'm not patronizing you," Deborah said soothingly. "Come on." She rattled the china dish. "Down the hatch."

Jack pushed the dish of pills away from him.

"There was nobody at the station," Catherine said.

"Don't be stupid," Jack said. He stood up. He'd shed the old-man shuffle, the saggy, beaten posture she'd seen when she'd come in.

Outside, tires hummed over the old cobblestone street. The coffeemaker let out an exhalation of steam. Deborah scraped her chair away from the table. "Can I speak to you for a moment?" she asked, meaning Catherine. She opened the kitchen door and waited for Catherine to step through it.

"Don't worry," Jack said. "I'm calling Lenny." He was at the window, peering through the shade. "Everything's going to be okay."

"You are *not* calling Lenny. Take those," Deborah said, indicating the dish of pills. She picked up the cordless phone off the side table and used it to wave Catherine out of the room.

Catherine followed Deborah through the dining room, through the foyer, into the living room, where the fireplace had held the same bag of coal since Catherine was a girl. The furniture was formal: an armchair upholstered in silk, a cushioned bench by the leaded casement window. Marble-topped end tables were covered with her mother's fashion-history books. Deborah stood in the middle of the room, her arms crossed.

She hit the talk button on the phone. Jack's voice was tinny in the speaker: ". . . *right now, Lenny. She's here now,*" he was saying. "Jack!" Deborah shouted into the phone. "Hang up," she said. "Hang. The. Phone. Up."

Whoever he was talking to said: "*Christ.*"

Deborah switched off the phone. "See what's happening?"

"No," Catherine said.

"You know your father is sick?"

Catherine asked carefully: "How do you mean?"

"Your call put our treatment back *weeks*. Look"—Deborah raised both hands—"I know you're his daughter, and I'm not trying to interfere with that, but you can't joke with him. You can't *encourage* him."

"What treatment?"

Deborah went to the window and parted the heavy velvet curtains. Morning sunlight washed in. "His two friends were sent to quarantine. The police chief knew your mom, so Jack went to Riverside instead. I was the admitting nurse and put him on some pretty heavy mood stabilizers. We've been making good progress since. And now here you are and your presence is not . . . Like I said, your call set him back."

Catherine tried to piece together what she was saying.

"They were at a screening center," Deborah explained. "Your dad and his friends. Picketing, shouting craziness, paranoid stuff about the government. The police came and it got a little rough. Your father took a swing at a cop." She paused. "Obviously you can see him."

"You're a nurse? Are you *living* here?"

Brief pause. "No."

"No?"

Deborah took a quick breath. "The point is you can't encourage him. This idea that you're being tracked—"

"I probably am," Catherine interrupted.

Deborah's lips pursed, but before she could say anything, Catherine turned around and lifted her shirt. She lifted it high into her armpits, feeling the cool air on the tender skin of her scar.

"What am I looking at?"

Catherine let her shirt drop.

47

Catherine examined the pills in the kitchen. "What does she have you on?" She called out: "Dad?" Turned out he wasn't around the corner, washing dishes at the sink; the sink was empty, immaculate, the drain shiny and polished. She searched the empty dining room, the foyer; she called up to the second floor; she had a moment of panic thinking he'd left too. Slipped out the front door with Deborah. Chosen a new and improved life over helping his daughter. Then she heard movement below, footsteps and a rustling sound. A door off the kitchen led down into the cool, cavernous basement. She snaked past the ancient furnace, with its tentacle pipes and glass dials; passed the laundry room, where a neat row of detergent, bleach, fabric softener, and other supplies stood above the machines; and found her father in a space he had once talked about as a workshop, then a gym, but had only ever been used for wine storage, treadmilling, and, very occasionally, Ping-Pong.

He was sliding cardboard boxes marked XMAS SUPPLIES and empty wooden wine crates out of the way. He pushed his old treadmill up against the wall and rolled plastic sheeting around the Ping-Pong table in the middle of the cement floor. Picking his way around in his sandals and gold-toe socks, he hooked work lights into eyelets in the ceiling.

"Deb is wonderfully kind to me," Jack said, as if he'd heard her. "You should give her a chance."

"Seems like she's cleaned the place up."

"So?"

"What are those pills she has you on?"

"She doesn't *have* me on anything. Vitamins. Magnesium. A lightweight antianxiety. All of it quite voluntary. Did she go to her sister's?"

"She said you were in some place called Riverside?"

"Barely."

"You hit a policeman? At a screening center?"

He squinted as if trying to remember.

"And that's how you met. Is she your girlfriend?"

Jack smiled, a look of mischief on his face. "I know what you're thinking. But Deb's not DOH. I had her checked out."

"That's not what I was thinking."

His eyes went up into the cobwebbed corners of the ceiling. He let out a deep, exasperated breath. "I'd just about written you off and here you are."

"I'm sorry for not returning your calls. I said I was sorry, didn't I?"

"But it's not to bond with dear old Dad. You need my help." She watched him billow a plastic sheet over the Ping-Pong table and smooth it out with the back of his hand.

She realized what he was doing. "Wait," she said. "Down *here?*"

"Where would you prefer?" It was cool in the basement, but sweat had dampened and wrinkled his shirt. Ancient paint peeled and flaked from the ceiling in strips. Dust rode the air. "Lenny said it would be fine. Just get the room as sanitary as possible."

"Lenny is . . ."

"A terrific surgeon. Used to work for Richmond Presbyterian," he said, and winked. "I've known him for years." His back had straightened. He was focused, his movements precise. "Cytofit, you said. And how long have you had it?"

"Four months."

"Catherine—*why* on earth?"

"I told you I had a cough. I'd run out of a screening center."

"You climbed out the bathroom window."

"I thought I was sick, and then this came along." She took a breath and decided that that was enough. The rest of it—Pursuit, the HideAway, Mercer, Chad—she would keep to herself. "Dad, are you *okay*?"

"The DOH is behind this somehow, duck. You realize that, right?"

"Are you?"

"People can get rid of their MED cards. But what about something under your skin?"

She closed her eyes. She had to believe that he was. "It stings," she said. "Something might be . . . wrong with it?"

Jack tore a length of duct tape off a roll with his teeth. "Could be," he said, and taped one edge of the plastic sheet to the underside of the table. He stepped around to the other side and pulled the sheet flat. "Don't worry, duck. It's all going to be fine."

Staring at the table's warped wooden legs, Catherine badly wanted that to be true.

"You want one of your mother's Valiums?" he asked. "Sure you do. Let's get you one."

48

Jack led her upstairs. He cracked the shade in the foyer an inch and told her to keep an eye on the street. "What am I looking for?" she asked.

He disappeared to the second floor without answering. Catherine watched the early morning traffic roll by and wondered fleetingly if she was being selfish. Drugs or not, Deborah had clearly been taking care of him and suddenly here's Catherine flipping up her shirt. The look Deborah had given Catherine before walking out the door was not resentment or hostility but concern: *You're as crazy as he is.*

Maybe she was. Catherine thought of the table in the basement and endured an interval of doubt. Jack came down the stairs, his shirttail out, his thinning gray hair in a mussed cowlick above his head. He took a silver pill case out of his trouser pocket, slid the top open, and spilled a mix of white, blue, and pink tablets into his palm. "April was taking a lot of different things toward the end," he muttered. "Pink are amphetamine—you definitely don't want those. Take a white one. That's the Valium, I think."

"You think."

"Take one. It's fine."

49

Nostalgia washed over Catherine at the sight of the paved rear courtyard. She used to roller-skate here, turning tight figure eights between the house and the garage, letting the drain in the center slip between her skates. The garage opened like a breezeway to the alley. She remembered when her dad would roll both doors open and tinker with one of his MGs. *Dad, watch this*, she'd shout, turning on one foot, her arms spread for balance.

Today the garage was shut tight, the small, square windows coated in dust.

She descended the steps onto the heaved-up concrete, coarse weeds sprouting from the cracks.

Jack unlatched the gate just adjacent to the garage and a gray-haired, ponytailed man wheeled his motorcycle through. It was a faded-red Triumph, with a shallow-brimmed beanie helmet dangling from the handlebar. The man wore a chambray shirt wide open at the neck, and a gold hoop shone in his left ear. His leather shoulder bag sported a fringe of cowboy tassels. "Showtime, fella," he said.

"Lenny," Jack said, clapping him on the arm. "Good of you to come."

"*Good* of me. The manners on this guy," Lenny said, big eyes rolling around. "Is Mom home?"

Jack answered quickly, "I wish you wouldn't call her that."

"You're a grown man. Can't have your old lady telling you who you can't talk to on the phone." Lenny turned his long, wrinkled face to Catherine. His hair was matted and greasy from the helmet. He rocked the Triumph back on its kickstand. "I started some chatter about this thing on the boards," Lenny said. "There's a reason they put it in her lower back is the consensus." He screwed a finger into his palm; his nails were grimy. "We're wondering if they got it jacked into her spinal column somehow."

Jack swore quietly. "I said stay off the boards. I told you to keep—" He stopped himself, glanced up at Catherine, then went to the gate and looked both ways down the alley.

"Don't you worry, fella. IP address says I'm in Minsk." He turned to Catherine. "Your pop's a little paranoid, you know that?"

Catherine couldn't take her eyes off the crescents of dirt under Lenny's fingernails. "You're a surgeon?" she asked.

"Ha!" Lenny said, more of a bark than a laugh. "Is that what you told her? Gilding the lily aren't we, Jack? Sixteen years as an NP at Richmond Prez."

"We're not taking any risks here," Jack said, closing the gate and turning the bolt. "I'll be content just to look at the thing."

"*You* will. The rest of us want it in the bucket," Lenny said. He unlaced one of the motorcycle's panniers and tossed Jack a plastic drugstore bag packed with supplies. "Spin around and let me see it," Lenny said to Catherine, tightening his ponytail.

She backed up the steps to the door.

"It's okay," Jack said, scratching his chin—then he rubbed his eyes with both fists. "Lenny's being modest. I've known him a long time. He knows what he's doing."

"You got her on any kind of sedative?"

Jack nodded.

"Lemme see what you've done with the basement."

Catherine squared herself in the doorway. "Dad?"

Jack bent to pull a weed from the erupting concrete. He did it carefully, grasping the thing by its roots.

"Jack. Set the girl's mind at ease," Lenny said. "Remind her what the stakes are. Who she's in bed with."

50

There it was, the Valium beginning to work, a liquid calm rolling through her. Her father's footsteps moved to the base of the stairs, then crossed away to the foyer. He rustled the curtains on the windows, then came again to the stairs. Catherine took this hesitation, this indecision, as a warning. She held her bedroom doorknob in one hand, her cell phone in the other.

"He shouldn't be online yet," Jack said, as he climbed the stairs. "I told him to keep this quiet until we have it."

"Until you have it in the bucket," Catherine said.

"Look—I trust him. I trust Lenny."

Her cash lay in a pile underneath her clothes. She crouched to gather it into a neat stack. "Trust him all you want," she said.

"But he shouldn't have been on the boards with this," Jack said, standing in her bedroom doorway. "It's an unnecessary risk. With Pfizer, I waited till I had the evidence. You have to have the *evidence*. I told him."

"I thought you'd have someone competent. I thought—I don't know what I thought." She stuffed the bills in the pocket of her old jeans and pushed tickling strands of hair out of her face. She swayed, the Valium coming on really strong now—too strong, in fact, to be Valium.

"Duck . . . ," Jack started, but then lost his way, a boy's confusion in his wrinkled face. "Lenny's one of the good guys," he said. "One of the most committed I've met. It won't hurt, I promise. Then we'll take it apart, understand it, post the evidence, get moving."

Catherine felt like sitting down, but the only place was her bed, and she wouldn't be able to get up from that. She'd close her eyes, which suddenly seemed like an excellent idea. She'd let herself pretend this wasn't happening—which, come to think of it, *was* this happening? The room's colors had taken on a dreamy glow.

"Dad, that," she said, "was not actually Valium."

Lenny called up all the way from the basement: "*Donde esta* your video camera, fella?"

"In a minute," Jack said.

"Video camera?" Catherine realized she was speaking very slowly.

"You want to persuade people, you film the whole thing and post as quickly as you can," Jack said. "Link yourself to the evidence, so that if anything happens to you . . ." He licked his lips. "You make the information free. You let it spread and you put your name on it. People aren't so indoctrinated that they won't read about DOH wanting to implant every American and not sit up and say *no more.*"

She sort of bounced off her father trying to get out of the room. "I need to make a phone call," she said. *Frances*, she thought. *Call Frances.* The only person she could think of. "Can you—" She caught a view of her clownish stagger in the room's full-length mirror. "Can you move out of the way?" But by the end of her question, she'd sunk to her bed and closed her eyes for what was supposed to be a trial run.

"It could be a long time, duck," her father said. "Pfizer took six years. Deb'll understand that and she's patient. She's been patient with me. There's enough money."

"Was it some kind of a sleeping pill? Just tell me." She opened her eyes as wide as they would go. He was still in her doorway. He flicked the light off. "Dad? Please don't do anything till I wake up. Don't let that guy—"

"Shhhh."

"Please." Her vision steamed over. He turned away and closed the door.

51

Her sleep was thick but shallow, a bog she'd rolled into. She reached for her phone. She slapped her palm along the surface of the night-stand. She found the wall and the headboard, and then the edge of the mattress. Then she saw the phone on the floor, and she let gravity do its thing, sliding down off the side of the bed, and suddenly, painlessly, she was sitting on the rug in the room, phone in hand.

She found the name she wanted and listened to the ring. Four rings. Five rings.

"Long time no speak."

"Frances."

"Thanks for your concern, by the way."

Now that Catherine was off the bed, she desperately wanted to be back on it. "Can you help me? I need your help."

The phone let out a mournful tone signaling the battery was going.

"I don't *care* about you and Mercer."

The phone's battery was at 4 percent. She focused on her legs and feet, trying to get them under her so she could stand. "Rich- mond. I'm in—"

"Know what happened to Laird? Deported to *Scotland*. I can't sleep."

"Frances—" Impossible. Her head was too dizzy. She settled again on the floor.

"To Glasgow, Catherine." Frances's voice caught. "Where there are fully guys who want to *kill* him."

Catherine spoke as clearly as she could. "My dad gave me a sleeping pill, and I'm having a hard time—"

"Your *dad*? You're where?"

"Richmond," she said. She closed her eyes. "I need help."

No response.

The house was quiet, this big old house all around her that should have been haunted but wasn't. She listened to it.

She worked her eyes open. The phone was dead.

52

Probably Ambien, Catherine told herself, just something to knock Mom out, and how hard could that have been really, with all the wine she drank? So Catherine could fight this thing with a bit of concentration, with a solid application of her will. She could handle herself on drugs. She'd taken enough of them in college—weed mostly, but prescriptions too. Once she'd driven back to Vassar from a party in Manhattan, so stoned the Taconic spread from six lanes to ten. But she'd kept right, kept to fifty miles an hour, the windows open, taking lungfuls of the cool Hudson Valley air, and made it to campus in one piece. So that's what she did now—she filled her lungs, she concentrated on moving herself out of the bedroom and stepping as quietly as she could onto the empty second-floor landing. Balance was tricky; she'd have it and then lose it, like a drunk, finding herself four feet to the left. Even keeping her movements slow, she made more noise than she wanted to, the century-old floorboards advertising her progress. She rested at the top of the stairs, both hands spread on the banister, staring down into the lifeless air below. She expected to see both men hurtling up toward her. But there was nothing but the cut lilies on the landing, the half-circle table, and the porcelain bowl. To her right, the bathroom was hot sun bouncing off tile—a brightness and warmth that barely reached her. The house was dark, cool, dumb, an old dead box. A musty smell came off the tapestry draping one wall.

She rubbed the goose bumps off her arms and eased her way down the stairs, sliding one shoulder along the wall. With each step she gained confidence. She felt more assured, positively graceful in her movements. There no longer seemed a danger of falling down. She focused on the floor below, on the big wooden door, on the bolt she was almost certain she could turn; she'd get herself outside onto the street and just walk in any direction until she found a safe place to lie down.

And then? Her brain was quiet on the question, easing over the troublesome details of money, friends, support. Coming to Richmond had been yet another mistake, she admitted to herself. How many could she make? Once she was out of that door, she had no idea where she was going next, but she'd figure it out.

Hopeful as she felt, when Lenny ambled toward her with a needle, she found she could barely raise a limp hand. He stepped around her, clamped her high on the arm, and sank the needle into her skin. She heard a whimper, then a sigh, then realized she'd made them. She fell to the welcoming floor.

53

They carried her like a sack of grain down the basement stairs, Jack on her wrists and Lenny hoisting her ankles up into his armpits. She was on the verge of losing consciousness—welcoming that pleasant gloomy cool of not caring what happened next—when one of them stumbled, yanked her, and something in her shoulder let go. The pain periscoped to the surface. "Ow," she said, or tried to say; her voice came out barely above a whisper. The men cursed and grunted and heaved her up onto the Ping-Pong table. Air shot through her lips with the impact, and Catherine blinked into the glaring work lights, her mouth hanging open like a decked fish's. Gradually her air came back, but her body was slow; sensations crept to her muddled brain. They rolled her over, and Jack used something slippery and soft—neckties, she saw—to secure her wrists to the table's legs. She listened to the sound of her shirt being scissored away. She felt the basement air pillow onto her skin. Fingertips sheathed in rubber slid under the waistband of her jeans. "Leave them," Jack said, but in a moment, they were cut away too. Lenny's ripe leathery odor enveloped her face. She couldn't move her head but had a pretty decent view of a length of floor, from the shiny plastic immediately below her to the spread pegs of the camera tripod, to the dusty join with the stone wall. Her dad's sandaled feet stepped in and out of view. Something cold was dabbed onto her skin. There was a needle prick, a wooden numbness, a barely detectable dorsal tugging. Minutes of this passed. Blood spotted the plastic at the very periphery of her vision.

"Jesus, Lenny. I think she's awake. You said—"

"It's a deep twilight. Don't worry. Possible to get some music down here? Something heavy? Mahler?"

"Look at the blood. Are you focusing on what you're doing?"

"Swing in here with some gauze."

Catherine watched her father's feet move reluctantly from their post behind the camera.

"Just blot, don't wipe. Like that. Right."

"Where is it, Lenny?"

"That's the question, fella. Where you hiding, little bastard?"

There was no pain, only that odd tugging. "There she is," Lenny said. "Deeper than I thought. And look how they got it embedded in here."

"What an awful lot of blood," Jack said in a weak voice.

Rivulets ran in the folds of the plastic sheeting. Soaked wads of gauze plopped like plucked flowers into her field of vision. Catherine closed her eyes.

"See? They worked it in there pretty good."

"I have no idea what I'm looking at. How much blood can a person lose?"

"You'd be surprised."

A person. Her back was gone—dead numb—but the rest of her still sent sensation along to her brain, and Catherine realized in a slow-reel way that she was painted with blood, that her stomach had adhered wetly to the table. She heard the pitter-pat of more spilling down.

"Tough to maneuver in here, fella. See the musculature around the vertebrae? They've got it rooted in deep. You need to know what you're doing in here. Like defusing a bomb."

"God, Lenny, maybe you should stop."

Stop, Catherine wanted to say. A simple thing—tongue touching the bridge of her mouth, lips coming together—but she just couldn't get the word out. She only felt her breath on her teeth.

"I'm just telling you. They've put it in here for a reason. I don't have the instruments to do this without damaging—"

Her father's voice rose in pitch. "You said you knew what you were doing!"

Lenny was calm. "I do. I can. I know enough to say if I cut around this thing there's a chance the girl doesn't get off the table."

"You said you could get it out without hurting her."

The only pain was in her shoulder, a hot pulsing that helped keep her awake. In the region of her back there was this strange pressure and warmth, like a heating pad laid across her. She listened to the drips and watched the streams of blood in the plastic run together and widen.

The footsteps were dreamed, she thought. The sound of a door broken off its hinges. The commotion and shouting. The men, suddenly crowding the room. The loud punctuation: *pop, pop, pop.* Two bodies slapped down heavily on the plastic.

She worked her eyes open and saw her father doing a sort of sideways crab scuttle across the floor.

Boots. Many sets. Her father was prodded with a booted foot. A bleat of static. "We're clear."

Another voice. "Two of them. Both down."

The men squelched across the plastic. And then there were more, white-suited medics with a folding stretcher. She watched the blood soak up into her father's shirt. She was aware of someone standing over her, applying pressure to her back.

A man's face in a respirator leaned in close. "She's conscious. Can you hear me?" The man pulled his respirator off. "Christ, what a mess."

Her body was covered with a cloth and she was loaded sideways onto the stretcher. Foam blocks were nestled against her ears. Straps held her down, the pain in her shoulder keeping her head clear. It was an awkward climb up the basement stairs, but they did their best to keep her horizontal. The door had been knocked down, and both sides of the garage were up. She saw the MG, the windshield covered in dust. Both front tires were flat.

Out in the alley behind the house, they slid her into the bay of an ambulance. One of the medical techs looked up from a small screen and told the others her blood type and then the name of what had been in Lenny's syringe. Someone asked if she was going to make it. By that point they'd hit her with someone else, another needle burrowing into her arm, and her vision was now pinning down to black, but she thought the reply was hopeful. Something like: "Yes. Tell him yes." It was the medical tech speaking. Saying something reassuring: "Tell him we've got her. Tell him she's secure."

QUARANTINE

54

Inches from Catherine's face, the tiled wall. She studied the lanes of gray grout, then turned her head to a milk-white nylon hospital curtain and let her vision blur and focus like a camera finding its range. It took an unnatural effort to get her legs to move, but gently, an inch at a time, she scissored them beneath the cool length of sheet. The effort made her dizzy and knocked her into unconsciousness. She dreamed of her legs turning useless, like a pair of heavy pylons, her arms dangling like ropes. Then she woke and moved them again, and again they resisted—a terrifying feeling.

I'm okay. Catherine forced the thought, drove it through the chemicals waterlogging her head—sedatives, painkillers, god knows what else.

55

She was dimly aware of the IV feeding into her arm, of the ticking and beeping of monitors around her. Dimly aware of the smells—disinfectant, vomit, human waste—that drifted into her room whenever a nurse unlocked it and stepped through.

The nurses floated in and out without speaking. They wore masks, checked her chart, and added meds to her IV drip. Only her doctor, a man with RAJANI on his name tag, perched on the edge of her bed, pulled his mask to his neck, and talked to her with such an even temper, with such routine, unforced optimism, that it often took her until he was gone to process what had been said. She was in Newark quarantine, in a special research wing off the main wards. She'd been admitted in very rough shape: under deep sedation, her back a bandaged mess, her shoulder dislocated, zero reflexes from the waist down.

"The paralysis made me think nerve damage—you were badly sliced up, you'd lost *quite* a lot of blood," Rajani said.

Paralysis. She tried to sit, but she couldn't get her legs under her. Rajani said she should stay just as she was. "You've been through a trauma. You need to rest." When her reflexes were back, a regimen of physical therapy would get her strength up. She'd be walking around in no time.

"How long . . . ?" A dry whisper.

"Shhh," Rajani said, pushing her hair out of her face. "We'll talk when you're ready."

Before she could muster the energy to say anything, one of the silent nurses hovering behind him injected something into her IV line. Sleep folded over her.

56

She dreamed of the prep-league semifinal, senior year, one-hundred-degree heat, and the fast, tough St. Mary's team widely considered the favorite. Catherine's St. Ann's squad evened the score to 2–2 in regulation and then she struck the game-winning assist in sudden-death overtime on a fast-break cross from the corner that had found her teammate's stick. She saw the ball billow the net and collapsed on the sideline, emptied of everything but relief. Teammates piled on top of her, crushing the air out of her chest—and the relief turned to joy. They'd *won*. The sun on her, the cheers. The feeling of being part of something. The sky an endless banner of blue.

57

She dreamed of her father seizing her by the arm, Lenny with that
syringe. She saw the plastic sheeting glittering under the work lights.
She saw Lenny scissor her clothes away. Her naked skin was white
and she saw the blade poised to part it like paper. *Stop*, she wanted
to say. But Lenny had already made his incision and through the
blood, down past pink banks of muscle, there was the device, buried
deep in the lightless core of her, nestled there half-hidden, like a
scorpion in a shoe.

58

Catherine woke and took in the gleaming table, nearly within arm's reach of the bed. Set on top was a shallow tray with a box of latex gloves, a vacuum-packed thermometer, and a glass vase filled with marbles and an arrangement of daisies. Fake daisies. Threading on the petals.

Rajani raked the nylon curtain back, revealing to Catherine the dimensions of the room she was in. It was a large space of floor-to-ceiling tile, harshly lit by circular wall sconces. At the corner of the room, beyond another hospital bed—empty—were two port-hole-shaped windows. Through one of them she could see an empty, muddy field crisscrossed by cement pathways.

Rajani took a firm grip on her arm and helped her sit, dropping her legs over the edge of the bed. The room lurched. Her hand crashed onto the steel table.

"Easy, easy. Now take a couple of steps—just down the length of the bed." He rolled her IV tree with her as she shuffled her bare feet. The tile was cold under her toes and the air tickled her bare butt. Her legs were so *heavy*. Her back ached.

"Now . . . backward. Two steps and you're in bed," Rajani said, helping her, settling her. "Good, that was good."

Catherine held on to his sleeve. Rajani was young—in his early forties maybe—and his eyes were kind, concerned, big as coins.

"How long have I been here?"

He disconnected the IV from the needle feeding into her arm and then, with a brisk motion, slid it out of her vein. Cotton ball. Tape. "Few weeks," he said.

Weeks. She licked her cracked lips. "My dad," she asked him, speaking through heavy breath. "Do you know what . . . happened? Is he . . ."

"He's alive," Rajani told her, and his face widened with a smile. A cheerfulness lay just beneath the surface. "I'm allowed to tell you that."

She released his sleeve. She heard her father's voice in her head: *It's all going to be okay.* She heard the gunfire *pop-pop-pop* and saw him crab-scuttle across the floor.

"You're comfortable here? It's not such a bad room?"

It was—floor-to-ceiling tile cruelly gleaming.

A small device on Rajani's hip beeped at him; he unholstered it and read something on its screen. "Sorry—other patients." He held her wrist, timed her heart rate against his watch, and then jotted a notation on the device with a stylus.

"Please stay," she said, no louder than a whisper.

Rajani shook his head. The porthole windows spotted with rain. He tore open the wrapping on a damp inch-square piece of micro-fiber, unpeeled one side, and stuck it to the inside of her arm. The fiber adhered to her skin; it tingled, then went hot. "A dermapatch," he explained. "The meds'll wear off. This will help."

The fiber darkened and swelled like a sponge. Almost immediately her body turned heavy, the light in the room soft. She heard the door close. The lock turned.

59

She woke staring at a pitcher of water and a tray of food—a crescent-shaped slice of ham, a small pile of baby carrots, a shallow dish of fruit salad. She realized how hungry she was. Also how much everything hurt. Her head throbbed. A rash of soreness ran along her back and legs.

She pushed herself up to a seated position, wincing, crying out as her weight shifted to her tailbone. With great effort, sweat beading at her temples, she turned her body clockwise and swung her feet off the bed. Perched sideways, smelling the mustiness of the sheets, a blanket of pain on her back, the overhead lights throbbing behind her eyes, she pulled the food tray to her and immediately drank half of the water pitcher, drenching her hospital gown. She gasped for air. The water felt so cool going down her throat. She felt the throbbing start to quiet. Then quickly, ravenously, she ate the food. All of it, every bite. Completely tasteless, but she didn't care.

Done, the water gone, she hung her head, closed her eyes, and felt the pain subside further. Tried to think. The IV was out of her right arm. The dermapatch on her left was dry, just a gray square that peeled easily away. She flicked it to the floor and rubbed the tender skin beneath it. The privacy curtain was gathered in deep folds beside the bed. Perhaps fifteen feet away, four steps, was the heavy steel door the nurses came through. It was fitted with a small window, through which she could see a corridor. Another door, standing open, led to a bathroom. Lipstick cameras aimed down at her from the corners of the ceiling.

Gingerly, she slid off the bed, bracing herself on its frame, and reached for the rolling IV tree for support. She tried not to cry out at the needling pains as her legs took her weight. Fighting each foot forward felt like wading through hip-deep mud—but she could do it. She was stronger than she expected. She reached the door and pressed her face to the window, looking both ways down the deserted corridor. The handle was firmly locked. She turned and passed her bed and made her way to the sealed porthole windows at the other end. One window revealed that field, pitted and rock-strewn. At the far end a lit security tower. The other had a different view: of single-story concrete buildings separated by muddy lawns, scraggly box hedges, and maple trees, the leaves starting to turn yellow and red. The flare of color, the change of season: it registered as a dull shock. The light was low and tinged with rose—dusk, she guessed. The only human beings she saw were a pair of men in bright orange jumpsuits gathering litter with pincers along a high razor-wire fence. She rapped the glass, but they were too far away to hear.

She turned and crossed the room again, her legs loosening with every stride. She did four laps and then, needing to pee, entered the small bathroom.

The mirror above the sink showed a gaunt, ghostly-pale figure. Her vision blurred with tears. She turned, gathered her gown, sat on the toilet, and ran her fingers across the swath of bandages covering her lower back. How *many* weeks had she been here?

A nurse opened the door to the corridor and stared openly at Catherine on the toilet. "I need you back in bed," she said through her mask.

"Just a minute," Catherine said.

The nurse stood there watching her.

"Where's the doctor?" Catherine asked. She stood and flushed.

The nurse prepared another dermapatch as Catherine moved to the bed. She peeled the plastic backing and took Catherine's left arm by the wrist. "Wait, do I need that?" Catherine said. "What's *in* it?" No response, and the moment the fiber hit her skin, it began to swell. She fought the chemicals as long as she could but eventually the fatigue socked her backward, and down she went into the pillow.

60

Rajani entered the room with a tablet, lit with a pixelated, pea-soup image. "I was able to upgrade the resolution on the imaging." He pointed at the corner of the screen. "That's an electrical lead, like a defibrillator—the smallest I've ever seen." His finger slid to another part of the image: a cloudlike wash of lighter green. "And this is a quite sensitive array of biometric sensors. The sensors are designed to pick up the presence of the virus and the lead delivers a targeted pulse to your spine. I can't tell from the images but a microchip, I'm guessing, sends a radio frequency or satellite signal so they know where you are when your legs go out from under you." He studied her expression intently.

Catherine was silent, trying to pick through what he'd said.

"To collect you. To isolate you until the paralysis wears off and you're no longer contagious."

She rubbed the sleep out of her eyes and noticed the hospital gown was gone. She wore beige sweatpants and a matching long-sleeve T-shirt. A pair of sneakers were laid on the floor.

"Can't spread TX if you can't move," he said. "Completely radical solution. A little blunt, of course—and I have some questions. You can't have this happen while driving down the interstate. And how do you *distribute* it? How do you put something like this in a patient's back? How did they talk *you* into it?" He crouched to face level and spoke quietly: "Did they pay you? I'm really asking because traceable MED cards were a hard enough sell. Big Brother and all that."

Her mind was still furiously scanning his sentences, as if they were obscure lines of poetry or a passage from a difficult book.

"Of course, if you don't have close to one hundred percent distribution, it won't stop much."

She surprised herself by taking his hand in hers. Rajani's skin was warm and dry. He stiffened at the contact—he had no gloves on—but he didn't pull away.

"Can you . . ." She licked her lips. "Can you get it out of me?"

"No," he said quietly. "The device is, well . . . think of it as a fishhook. Those sensors are tamper-proof. Your father's friend activated them simply by getting close."

Fishhook. She saw that cruel shape.

"Totally unethical that you weren't told—that I wasn't told. But the good news is someone in Washington wants you well, wants you up and about." He gestured for her to sit up. He reached for her legs and she cried out as he swung them roughly off the bed. "Time to start PT. I said that you can't rush a recovery, but they're firm that you should get moving."

"Who?" she managed to ask. "Who is?" And when Rajani didn't answer, the names came out quickly, like an incantation, as if by saying them she might make them appear: "Mercer Kerrigan. Chad Bonafleur. Sandy Robeson."

Rajani pumped sanitizer out of the wall-mounted dispenser and smoothed it between his palms.

"You don't know them?"

A nurse was standing inside the door, stationed behind a wheelchair. Rajani dismissed her with a flick of his hand and helped Catherine into the sneakers. "I have bosses like everyone else."

He wheeled her out of the room and down the corridor. The monotonous gleaming tile of the hallway was broken with banks of windows. Through them groundskeepers in boots rolled new sod across black mud. The floor and walls smelled of disinfectant. There was also the stench of bodies, which spiked as she passed half-open treatment rooms. Catherine caught glimpses of other patients through windows set in doors—a man in a canted bed with a breathing tube in his mouth, a woman beneath a plastic tent.

"I'd like to use a phone," she said—wondering even as she said it who she could call.

Rajani shook his head.

"Please," she said.

Rajani hushed her, and seeing she was only getting more upset, took from his jacket pocket a picture of a smiling young girl.

"It's my daughter, Mina. Age ten," Rajani said. "You remind me of her."

She couldn't see how. Pencil-straight hair, braces on her teeth, a plastic flowered barrette in her dark hair.

They reached an elevator. Stationed beside it was a uniformed guard with a helmet and an automatic rifle. He made only the slightest move to give Rajani and Catherine space as the doors slid open. Catherine turned to look at his weapon, the stenciled number on the curved clip, the buffed polish of the wooden stock.

Rajani pressed a button for the second floor. The guard entered the elevator with them as the doors closed. The doctor glanced nervously at him, but he was unresponsive, staring straight ahead, as if carved out of wood. "Her mother died when she was eight," Rajani said. "You can imagine how traumatic—hearing her cough all night long, watching them carry her away. But she's back to her old self now. A *voracious* reader." He took the picture. "What did you read when you were ten? Zombie novels for girls? Did they have those? Cute boys climbing up out of their graves to take you to prom?"

61

"There's nothing wrong with you," the physical therapist, Doris, told her. She was a small-town Kentucky girl with a crucifix around her neck and bobbed brown hair. "You been in bed too long is all." She said this after dropping Catherine flat on the floor mat like a wrestler, forcing her limbs into unnatural positions, and grinning whenever she cried out in pain.

The sessions went on for a week. She didn't see Rajani again during that time, but nurses came to put her in the wheelchair and roll her through the facility's corridors. And it was on that route, past two closed doors with red EXIT signs, that Catherine began to fantasize about springing out of the wheelchair, crashing through one of those doors, just as she had at Chad's office. She wondered how far she could make it. Guards were all around the clinic and the quarantine grounds—roving pairs of men in plastic suits that ballooned cartoonishly in the breeze. Some of them wore respirators; all carried automatic rifles high on their chests, the muzzles aimed at the dirt.

But, of course, she couldn't run. She still walked with a coltish limp. There was a strange lassitude in her too—as if they were giving her something to make the time pass. Something in the tasteless vegetable soup, the rice pilaf, the small squares of roast chicken, the cups of fruit salad she ate sparingly, only enough to beat back her hunger. She passed meditative hours by her small windows, idly doing knee

243

bends as Doris had instructed her to, watching patients released
from the concrete ward into a fenced recess yard. She thought about
what Rajani had said, going over and over his sentences. *The lead de-*
livers a targeted pulse to your spine. They know where you are when your
legs go out from under you. Can't spread TX if you can't move.

The other patients had beige sweat suits like Catherine's. They
stood smoking cigarettes, pacing, or doing nothing at all. She longed
to be with them, to take some fresh air into her lungs. She asked
Doris if she could try walking the grounds. Instead Doris gave her
a posture ball and rubber straps and ordered her to do stretching
exercises in her room. That was her last session. The next four days
she spent alone, visited only by nurses who wouldn't speak. Then just
before dawn, through slitted eyelids, she woke to discover Rajani at
her bedside. "Shh," he said, a finger to his lips, briefly laying the back
of his hand on her forehead. He hadn't shaved, or, from the look of
it, slept. His jacket was misbuttoned and dingy around the neck. His
eyes were bloodshot. His breath was bad.

"What—what happened to you?" Catherine said. She switched
on the panel light above her head and saw that his left eye was swollen, his eyebrow split and crusted over with dried blood.

Rajani looked over his shoulder. "It doesn't make any sense.
Your existence is not a secret. You're in the *papers*, for goodness' sake.
They're idiots if they think people won't find out—"

Voices and heavy footsteps in the corridor. Her door burst open.
Two armed guards came in wearing full-face respirators. Rajani
put his hands in the air and stepped away from Catherine's bed.
"She's still my patient," he said. "She's still my patient and I'm
responsible—" His face clenched in pain when one of the guards
drew his arms down and behind his back and cinched his wrists
with a plastic tie.

Catherine could only watch, horrified. Rajani's hard look told
her to stay quiet. The guards took him away and locked her door.

62

Despite the slanting afternoon glare she could see into the back-seat of the open Audi. She could see a cuffless trouser leg hiked up to reveal a sock of iridescent silk, a brown leather shoe flat on the upholstered cabin floor. She heard the nurse reverse the wheelchair into the alcove behind her and she heard the glass doors cycle shut.

Catherine lingered there at the top of the clinic's four broad cement steps. No one was forcing her down to the parking lot, no nurse or armed guard, and she gazed past the yellowing lawn to the low, climbable concrete wall that ringed the lot. She couldn't be sure of her legs, that they would let her run and climb, nor of what lay beyond that wall: patrolled quarantine grounds, or New Jersey industrial tracts, a no-man's land that surrounded her for miles. Not a hopeful prospect. And even if she got through it all there was nowhere—truly nowhere—for her to go.

Still, it was thrilling not to have anyone forcing her into Mercer's car. It was thrilling to be outside after so many weeks. Early November, the nurse had told her. Catherine felt the afternoon chill through the soft cashmere sweater she'd been given to wear. A fast-moving cloud tracked low on the horizon. A skeletal tree was planted in the pale grass, gaudy leaves around its trunk like a dropped skirt.

She descended the clinic stairs toward the car and lowered herself into the warmth inside.

Without so much as an exchange of glances with Mercer, she leaned her head against the headrest. She recognized the driver— his thick neck, the fingerless gloves on the wheel.

"Welcome back," Mercer said, a line perhaps intended as a joke, but he didn't laugh and neither did Catherine.

Quarantine perimeter was a series of reinforced steel fences adorned with biohazard signs and notices that read PROPERTY OF THE UNITED STATES OF AMERICA. Mercer handed Catherine's discharge papers to the guards. The trunk was checked. The undercarriage inspected with mirrors. Eventually the gates were rolled out of the way, the bollards sunk flush into the surface of the road. As they drove over them and sped around a canted exit ramp, Mercer said, "How about 'You're welcome'?"

It wasn't so bad, the leather seat cradling her, the calming sensation of speed, the faint curiosity about where she was being taken. *You're welcome.* She glanced at Mercer and saw that he was nicely dressed. Gray suit, white shirt, pocket square.

"Was the rescue exciting?"

She kept her face as expressionless as possible.

"I missed you, Cate. Frances was sure you were dead. She bet me fifty bucks. I told her they just needed to fix you up."

She felt him smiling at her. "You're angry," he said with genuine surprise. "You're angry at *me*? I'm the reason you're alive. Chad wanted to let you bleed out on that table in Richmond and *then* send the team in. Easy solution, he said. The man's lack of vision never ceases to amaze—"

She hit him. She used the side of her hand and aimed for his chin but caught him awkwardly in the neck. She connected hard. He guttered with surprise.

"Jesus," he said, coughing.

The driver swerved in his lane, cocking his head to see them in his rearview.

Still coughing, Mercer tried to put his hand on Catherine's arm, but she slapped him away. The sight of a blooming rosy mark on his neck produced a snaking sensation of pleasure down through the core of her.

"I know how it works," she said.

He made a pained face, and they rode in silence for a few minutes. Catherine felt her heart rate slow. Out the window was a slope of hunkered shrubbery and fast-food trash. An exit sign passed, its letters taped over, the ramp blocked off by sawhorses and traffic cones. There was no Manhattan skyline in view, just cement overpasses, an array of tapered smokestacks, the pinpoint lights of a power station.

Mercer drew a folder out of the back pocket of the driver's seat and laid it on her lap.

"What's this?"

"Are you going to hit me again?"

Inside she found several pages, the top three full of crabbed, dense type: the original release forms she'd signed in Robeson's office. She passed a finger over her signature, big and looping at the bottom of each page. Some lines on page two had been highlighted in yellow. A series of words inside a long paragraph about possible side effects. The words were: "back pain, stiffness, temporary loss of motor control."

"You knew you were getting a prototype," Mercer said. "You knew there were risks. You'll look sort of foolish saying otherwise." He put that simply, touching the edge of the folder, his fingers close to her leg.

"I'm not talking about a side effect."

"You know what you're talking about? Your expert medical

opinion has been brought to bear?" He gently massaged his throat. "From what I understand, and that's about twenty percent of what the lab guys tell me, there *is* an issue with your device. Something electrical. Nothing to get panicked about. The biosensors are functional, the antiviral's there, the deployment trigger works. You're still protected from TX. And the newer version has the fix, so we're fine."

"I was *paralyzed*—"

"It's harmless unless someone goes digging around in the old body cavity—that's what they tell me. It's been agony waiting for you to get better. But all's well: Acetor has the equipment to swap it out safely. A fifteen-minute procedure. Outpatient stuff. We should thank your dad for alerting us to the problem." Mercer avoided Catherine's gaze. "I like those guys—the lab staff at Acetor. Grounded. Not the best-looking group—fatties, half of them, and you should see the junk they eat, the doughnuts, but they'll stand there utterly focused, like Zen masters, working a remote arm that moves an invisible wire one micron to the left. All to make the world a better place. Compared to your average Pursuit member? Who nets money out of the air for eight hours and calls it hard work? The boys who built the miracle in your back have actual skills, not just Daddy's connections, good looks, a wicked short game. Know what I'm saying?"

She shook her head.

"Sure you do. The wealthy are cowards and criminals. By and large. These guys are different. Do they need to shoot people to feel good about themselves? Put a gun in their hands, they'd probably hand it back to you."

A dull smog descended on the highway. "Where are we going?" she finally asked.

"We need to get you in front of a camera," Mercer said. "Prove you're alive, healthy, mark your triumphant return to society. Back in the public eye, Miss Duval—how does it feel? How do *you* feel? I'll serve up the questions. We've got everything at the new HideAway: camera, lights, a few reporters. Sandy will give his medical opinion; then you'll answer a few questions, then we'll chopper you to Acetor for the swap-out. Did you see the *Times* piece? Probably not." He pointed at the folder.

She returned to it and found a news story dated two days ago. Headline: EXPERIMENTAL ANTI-TX DEVICE UNDER GOVERNMENT STUDY.

She scanned the first paragraph.

Department of Health scientists are examining an innovative implant at a quarantine facility in Newark, New Jersey, officials said today. Developed by Acetor, a little-known Cambridge, Massachusetts–based biotechnology company, the device, called Cytofit, is said to release combo doses of antiviral into the body the instant its carrier comes into contact with any strain of TX.

"Keep going," Mercer said when she looked up. "You're famous."

The Health Department statement follows reports that Acetor's test subject, Catherine Duval, 29, was kidnapped by what the DOH is calling a bioterrorist group. Sources at the DOH wouldn't comment on the motivations of the alleged kidnappers, who sustained injuries in a rescue operation and are being held at an undisclosed location. At a press conference today, Acetor's spokesperson, Mercer Kerrigan, freely speculated that there may have been a rival firm involved. "Our fear is that this was a case of corporate espionage," said Mr. Kerrigan. "The sophistication of our proprietary technology is unrivaled in the marketplace."

Mr. Kerrigan added that Ms. Duval may also have been

targeted because of her family connections. Jack Duval, Ms. Duval's father, made news two decades ago as the whistleblower in a landmark fraud case involving the drug company Pfizer. April Mayville, Ms. Duval's late mother, served as a top executive at her family's bathroom fixtures firm until the sale of the company ten years ago. She died in a car accident in December. Ms. Duval, along with her father, were the sole heirs to her estate.

Ms. Duval's wealth and well-known name are raising questions about Acetor's marketing plan for Cytofit.

Catherine stuffed the pages in the folder. She wouldn't read any more.

"Decent placement, but not A-one, so we've got to keep stoking the story. Tell the camera you're in great shape. The reporters will ask about the kidnapping—deflect those questions if you want. 'Too upsetting.' Say whatever. They won't push too hard. The key is to be positive, drop in the word 'immunity'—"

"You don't want to put me in front of reporters," she said quietly.

He leaned against the Audi's rear seat and regarded her. "Why not? You don't like the clothes I got you?"

The cashmere sweater. The suit pants one size too big, but a soft, expensive wool. "I'll tell the truth."

"The truth is for a few more weeks you're the only person in the world who has this thing. The truth is Acetor can distribute five thousand units by January. The truth is Pursuit members are clamoring for it. One guy who runs a private-equity shop is *requiring* his team get implanted. We're talking to the investment banks; we're talking to the big law firms. The Nursery has doubled our funding over the next twelve months and I'm confident we could get fast-track FDA approval and do an Acetor IPO as early as next year."

The driver pulled into the breakdown lane to pass a pair of trucks.

The guardrail was inches from Catherine's window—a blur of steel.

"I'll say what I know."

"What you think you know. What some good Samaritan doctor took it upon himself to tell you," Mercer said quietly.

"It doesn't protect you from anything."

"Go ahead. Honestly. Say that. Say paralysis. Give Chad the excuse he wants."

He brought a photo onto his phone's screen. It took Catherine a moment to understand what she was looking at—and then nausea rose through her. Dim light, a mass in the center of the frame: pulped scalp, crushed skull, scattered leaves, a patch of bare earth. Brain matter inside an ugly hole. "Fritz," Mercer said. He swiped left. A lit square of an apartment window, a woman visible through the glass. Dark hair to her jaw. "Krupa." He swiped again. Rajani seated at a steel table in a windowless room. His head tipped down, his face bruised and swollen.

Catherine turned to the window.

"And this one. Look."

She didn't want to but couldn't not. Her father on a hospital bed, his eyes closed, his skin gray, a tube running out of his mouth. Mercer slipped his phone into his jacket pocket. "He's alive by the way. I noticed you haven't asked."

Catherine kept her eyes on her lap, trying to chase the images Mercer had shown her out of her head.

"I'm about to hand him an elite clientele and he keeps sending me *pictures*. Because I've done what I said I'd do? Gotten us national attention? Created a bit of glamour around Cytofit? It's like he wishes it were still six months ago and no one had ever heard of his little investment. I keep reminding him all of this was his idea, but Chad's erased that bit of history from his memory. We're on the brink of this very big payoff and all he wants to talk about are loose ends: Frances, Laird, you."

Woods on either side of the car now. Steep banks of evergreens and a deepening gloom. Taillights jeweled in the murk.

"This summer he needed to hit a guy in the face to feel better. Now he's in this sort of stubbornly homicidal mood," Mercer said. "So do everyone a favor and make nice for the camera. Say how good you feel, how healthy you are. You wouldn't be lying. You *are* healthy."

"Where is Frances?"

"She'll be airborne by midnight. Scotland. Which, I know, I know—but she *wanted* to go. Misses Laird, she said. It's too bad. That girl is resourceful. Found targets for the new HideAway. Found this heavier-gauge plastic round that breaks the skin." Mercer rubbed his jaw. "But she's pregnant. Which is just all the more reason—"

"She's *what?*"

Mercer just nodded.

Catherine felt the nausea return. She thought of Frances's shrill cries carrying up through her bedroom floor. "Is it yours?"

He let out a dry laugh. "Oh right, sure. The immaculate conception."

She thought of how Mercer used to grip her by the neck; she thought of the time he forced himself on her. How much of everything between them had been about what he wanted, when he wanted.

She tried to make her voice steady: "This thing comes out of me tonight. And then I never see you again."

He shook his head, his gaze aimed forward through the windshield. "I need you visible, part of the message."

"Out of me tonight," she repeated. "Or I tell them."

"Tell them and you give Chad the excuse he wants." A long silence. "But yes, Acetor has the right equipment. So one demand granted," Mercer said, landing his hand on her knee and giving it a squeeze. "Give me a month. Even less: three weeks. Play ball."

They exited the freeway and began ascending a winding two-lane, the headlights sweeping through the dark. The driver took the turns at speed and Catherine had to brace herself to keep from sliding into Mercer. Her ears popped.

"Would it make you feel better," Mercer asked, "if you hit me again?"

63

The new HideAway was a log cabin perched on a sloping mountainside. Warm lamplight colored the wood-framed windows, tightly focused beams marked a gravel path leading from the small parking lot, and a stadium glow rose from the cabin's far side, where the land fell away. THE HIDEAWAY: MEMBERS ONLY read the discreet, brushed-aluminum sign. At least half a dozen cars were in the parking lot. Catherine followed Mercer out of the Audi, shivering in the cold. She could smell the turned earth and the fresh-cut timber.

"We can terrace a golf course down that way," Mercer said, crunching along the gravel path, gesturing with one flat hand. "Lose some trees, move a little earth. The permits won't come cheap of course." He smiled. "Frances would be rolling her eyes at me right now. She called this place a country club, like that's a bad thing. I told her there's no point trying to re-create the, you know, Unabomber charm of Fritz's HideAway. Better to go for comfort, full service. Anyway, Chad likes it. Gotta keep Chad happy! Helipad's up those steps." Catherine could see, terraced up high, the rotor and bulbous glass cabin of the helicopter. "New pilot. Remember the old guy?" Mercer asked. Catherine didn't respond. "I think Chad got him too. He won't answer his phone."

"Maybe *you* did."

Mercer laughed. "Come on. You think I'm capable of that?"

• • •

They entered a barn-sized room that smelled richly of wood polish and spruce logs. Opposite the entrance was a line of floor-to-ceiling windows overlooking a blazingly lit lawn; to the left, a stone hearth big enough to sleep in. A small group of men sat at the bar working their phones and eating stuffed olives off of toothpicks. The furniture—club chairs, trestle tables, floor lamps with parchment shades—had been pushed to the walls to make space for a podium, a lighting rig, and a video camera on a tripod. Catherine recognized Sandy Robeson studying a medical file in the corner. And she saw Chad bent over an end table. He was cleaning the disassembled parts of a shotgun.

"Mercer Kerrigan," one of the men at the bar said, yanking a notebook out of his rear pocket and wiping his mouth with a cocktail napkin.

"Hey, guys," Mercer said. "Thanks for coming. I know it's a long way."

"Can you confirm a few things?" The reporter triple-clicked a cheap pen. The others joined him—young men in jeans and wrinkled shirts with digital recorders and laptop bags slung from their shoulders.

There was one other journalist—he was older than the others, with a bald pate glowing under the soft light. He smacked down his empty glass. "Is this her?" he asked.

Mercer extended a protective arm across Catherine's body. "We're going to get started in a moment. Sorry about the distance, again, but Miss Duval's location is sensitive. I'm sure you can appreciate." Mercer smiled indulgently at Catherine, as if she were the one who had wanted to come out here. "Acetor's chief of research is going to speak first. And then—"

"Still say it was corporate theft?" the bald reporter asked. "There's no evidence that—"

"Attempted," Mercer interrupted. "And it wouldn't be appropriate for me to comment. Not while the investigation is ongoing."

"Your competition is saying you don't have anything."

"They would, wouldn't they," Mercer said. "Anyway, Miss Duval will speak after Dr. Robeson to give you her take on things. If she's game she'll answer a few questions."

"Glad you're okay, honey," the bald reporter said, tipping his head.

Blushing, grateful for that kindness, Catherine stared up into the rafters. They were heavy beams of salvaged oak—scorched, stippled by nails.

"Where are you with the FDA?"

"Ask the FDA."

The reporter who'd asked checked his watch, a chunky digital sports model. "I've got to file something."

"You'll have something."

In his corner Chad ran a greasy cloth across a two-pronged part and slid it into the shotgun's receiver. He then slotted the barrel into place.

"And who the fuck is that guy?" the bald reporter asked, pointing with his glass. "With the gun."

No one seemed to notice that Catherine had slipped away to one of the large windows overlooking the lawn. The grass sloped down the side of the mountain, terracing at the end, where, just barely, you could make out a fence behind a row of trees. You had to really squint through the haze to see, but there was a pair of bunkhouses set up just beyond.

"Acetor investor," Mercer said. "Touch eccentric. Leave him alone."

"Hey, buddy!" one of the young reporters said, shielding himself with his laptop bag. "Hey!"

Mercer froze; his jaw set. Chad had finished assembling his gun and was aiming at the group.

"Not loaded," he said.

The reporter scrambled for cover behind an armchair.

Click.

64

Mercer operated the camera, and Robeson took the podium. Chad leaned against the wall, the gun he'd cleaned aimed down at the wooden floor. The reporters, rattled from his stunt and visibly unnerved by his presence, took piecemeal notes. Robeson smiled at them and said that the patient was in fine health after her ordeal. He'd examined the lacerations in her back; he'd checked the functioning of the device; he'd reprimed its trigger. But of course he'd done none of these things. "She's feeling good and ready to return to normal life." Then he went on about how Cytofit had been shown to defeat exposure to TX virus in controlled settings. "Without going into details, I can reveal that our patient submitted herself to a contamination event several weeks ago, and I'm happy to report that she emerged from it perfectly healthy."

Contamination event. Catherine felt a beat of anger behind her eyes; her face warmed with it.

The room went silent. Chad had asked a question off-camera; he'd asked *her* a question. Passing in front of Robeson at the podium, in front of the reporters, the gun tucked under his arm, he asked it again: "I said: *want to do some shooting?*"

Catherine just stared at him.

"Chad," Mercer said, his voice low and tight.

"What? Think I'm going to hurt her?"

That got Catherine to her feet. Robeson's pages fluttered in a

draft as Chad opened the door to the rear deck. The reporters exchanged looks.

Robeson began to stammer: "Excuse the, ah . . . As I was saying
. . ."

Mercer started Catherine's way, but she'd already set off after
Chad.

Moving swiftly, she opened the door to the deck and let herself
outside, into the crisp chill. She followed Chad up a short flight of
stairs to a shooting platform where bright green empty shell can-
isters lay scattered at her feet. Lights cast a blanket haze down the
slope, which had been cleared and mowed and smelled of cut hay.
Bales were positioned on the grass here and there, for cover, presumably. She heard Mercer's footsteps on the deck. He hissed up at
them both: "The fuck are you doing?"

Chad ignored him. Catherine did too. Chad swept a tarp off a
spring-loaded arm and a crate of fist-sized sandbags. Set into the
wall there was a gridded speaker panel and a safe with a combination lock. He pressed a silver button on the panel and leaned in.
"Give me three guys." He then spun the combination, opened the
safe, and revealed stacked boxes of ammo.

The reply came out of the speaker: "*No shooting tonight.*"

Chad pushed the button again. "Three guys."

"C'mon," Mercer said, imploring now. "We have *people* here."

"Whose idea was that?"

There was silence for a moment. "*Our orders are no shooting tonight, sir.*"

"At least they call me sir." Chad sighed, loading his gun—five
shells out of a box. He casually aimed it at Mercer, then swept the
barrel toward the reporters watching through the windows. They
scattered out of sight.

"I need her inside," Mercer said carefully. "You know this."

"What do I know?" Chad said, and smoothly worked the pump.

"I know at this range Frances's new rounds would punch right through you."

Mercer scratched the top of his scalp.

"Get a sandbag on there," Chad said to Catherine.

Mercer turned with resignation. "Ten minutes, Chad. Then she talks on-camera."

Chad watched him go.

"Are you going to shoot me?" Catherine asked quietly.

"And ruin Mercer's press conference?"

"You already have."

Chad laughed. "He'll salvage it. Knowing Mercer. Pull the arm around till you hear a click."

Catherine examined the mechanism, yanked the spring-loaded arm, locked it in place.

"Good," Chad said.

A sandbag fitted neatly in a hollowed-out cup at the end.

"See the release line?"

Catherine did. She took the line and stepped away. Down the slope she saw men beyond the chain-link fence.

Chad noticed where she was looking. "Got 'em living down there. Packed in on bunk beds. Nicer than running around on the street. Except that would suggest they can run, and they definitely can't." He lifted the gun to his shoulder, squinting into the lights. "Pull."

Catherine tugged on the cord, the arm snapped around, and the sandbag sailed high. She clapped her hands over her ears. Chad pulled the trigger. One shot; the sandbag exploded.

"*You* could ruin it," Chad said. "But you won't. You'll go in there and calm everyone down and tell those guys that you're immune. That Cyto is the magic bullet they've been hearing about. Load me another."

Catherine slotted a sandbag in and worked the arm around. "Why would I?"

"Don't. I'd be fucking *thrilled*. Tell them what Rajani told you. Tell them how it works. We could start over. Make Cyto compulsory. Sock it into every American sent to quarantine. Pull."

The arm snapped. One shot. The bag burst into a cloud of sand.

"I've been dying to hit the reset button. But this thing has momentum now. Mercer is an irritatingly fortunate guy."

Catherine kept her eye on Chad's gun.

"Actually I don't give a shit about Mercer. Or Cytofit. This funk I'm in? My recent malaise? Your dad more or less diagnosed it. We're working on him and he says this really smart thing: *TX is a gift*. Takes away limits—even the pretense."

"Working on him," she repeated quietly.

"He's right. Pair of pliers in my hand. Couple of his fingernails on the floor. And no one's stopping me. Not the DOH suits in the room. Not the FBI heavy working the hose. Who could? The *press*?" He gestured dismissively inside. Catherine couldn't move. "I start thinking: *are* there limits? Killing Fritz was sort of an experiment, a test case. And what do you know? Nothing came of it. So I made a list. Your dad's at the top—but he's almost too easy. I'm thinking, what about an upstanding citizen like Krupa—what?—Chatwal? Her. And there's Rajani—a DOH *employee*. And that girl of his. Mina. How old did he tell you she was? Nine?"

"Ten," Catherine whispered.

"How about Frances and Laird? You can do anything you *want* in Scotland." Chad turned the gun on her. The barrels formed a perfect figure eight. "How about you? You think anything would happen to me? You think I'd be arrested?" He lowered the gun and notched another sandbag in the thrower. "Mercer's speech about ending fear sounds good, but I know better. Look at me. My life. What do I have to be afraid of? It's *boring*."

"I'd stop you," Catherine said. Tough talk that she didn't feel.

"Except you've never killed anyone. And that first time is hard.

You can't have second thoughts. You have to sort of leave yourself behind."

He offered her the gun. She took it from him. The grip was warm where he'd held it. The stock damp from his palm.

Catherine slid the grip and thumbed the safety flush. She aimed at Chad—who nodded. "*Yes.*" He grabbed himself. "Gets me hard just thinking about it. Pull the trigger and Mercer's big roll is over. A nice ending."

She remembered how the recoil felt, how to lean into the gun, prepare for the kick.

He shook his head. "But you're thinking about consequences. You're thinking: *what happens after?* You're thinking about the press guys inside, writing all of this up. The security guards Mercer's hired in the bunkhouse. You're wondering what they will do to you. Your mind is racing. You're starting to shake. You're letting it go on too long." He grabbed the barrel of the gun and jerked it to him, pulling her with it. He held the muzzle against his chest.

Catherine couldn't breathe, couldn't hold herself still. She was close enough to Chad to see his nostrils minutely flare, to see black chest hairs in the open neck of his shirt. A button, just above the gun muzzle, hung on a loose thread.

"I feel nothing," he said. "Not an ounce of concern."

Catherine let her finger rest on the trigger. She conjured an image to calm herself: wet road, driving too fast, throwing the wheel, the tree rising up.

Chad dipped his head, eyes closed.

She couldn't feel her hands, couldn't hold the gun steady. She heard footsteps behind her on the deck and a voice shouting her name. She glanced behind her.

And cried out. In that moment Chad had ripped the gun out of her hands, burning her fingers with the violence of it, and flipped the weapon around like a parade soldier. He aimed at her. Catherine took two fast steps away from him, then a third—into thin air. The steps. A sickening weightlessness as she fell down them, as Chad pulled the trigger, raking the air above her with plastic.

She was caught, lifted up, held. Arms clapped around her. Mercer's voice tinny in her ringing ears: "Stop. *Chad*—"

Chad's teeth were tight, his face a mask of adrenaline—but also pique, a kind of honed disappointment. He let the gun hang low. Mercer dragged Catherine away from him, then set her on her feet, turned her around, and shielded her with his body.

Chad blew his cheeks out. He worked the pump and sent an empty cartridge flying. He shook his head and then tipped it up to the light-scoured sky. He dragged the hand holding the gun across his mouth and seemed to get the better of some feeling. He spat at his feet, turned away from them, vaulted off the platform—a six-foot drop—landed lightly, and started descending the cut-grass lawn, the tidy hay bales in his path, the chain-link fence, the bunk-houses straight ahead. A man walking into his skeining breath, all intention and animal lope. The gun in his hand.

SCOTLAND

65

"I couldn't do it," Catherine told Laird as she buckled into the passenger seat of his Land Rover. "I wanted to. He *wanted* me to, but I couldn't."

Laird revved the engine out of its rough idle and dropped it into reverse. "Course you couldn't."

"What does that mean?"

"Means you're a fooking human being."

He'd grown his hair out straight and fair and wore a full beard that covered some of his knife-blade tattoo. She'd been so relieved to see him in the Edinburgh arrivals terminal that she'd dropped her bag and thrown her arms around his neck. He'd hugged her, but perfunctorily, telling her to hurry. The soldiers made him nervous. They stood around in camouflage uniforms, draining cans of lager or hazing the low-ceilinged corridors with their lit Marlboros. They made her nervous too.

At the parking deck, he'd scattered boys with jerricans and siphon tubes slung around their necks with a single barking shout. Then they were in his old boxy Defender, racing into an overcast Scottish morning. A tank sat at a rakish angle on a bank of overgrown landscaping; the airport, which hadn't had a single service open, just empty news sellers and shuttered cafés, was gray and dark to their left.

"How's Frances?" Catherine said. They got onto the M90 and

Laird took the speed up to pass cars and trucks, straining the engine.

"Bigger by the day. Cranky as fook." His voice softened. "Glad you're here, Cathy."

Catherine was too, in spite of the bleak roadside scenery: industrial buildings covered in graffiti against an ash-colored horizon, burned-out cars on the median. Or maybe because of it. Maybe the calm she was feeling—the rudimentary hope—came from what she saw; *this* was how wrecked and barren her life had become. Crows pocked a chain-linked field. A windowless van pressed by on their right, horn blaring.

Laird raced along for forty minutes, then he exchanged the motorway for smaller, snaking country roads. He negotiated tight, blind turns, towering roadside hedges blocking his view of oncoming traffic. He pointed out Ben Lawers, the mountain to the north, and told her in the spring it'd be blanketed in flowers. "This is still a fooking lovely country," he said. "Despite everything."

A nice ending, she thought.

"Cathy?"

66

At Lethendy, an honest-to-god castle, a sixteenth-century trape-
zoidal bulk of gray stone, Catherine read headlines whenever she
could. Whenever the maddeningly intermittent Internet service
worked. She searched "Cytofit" and occasionally came across the
quotes she'd given. Searched Rajani's name. Krupa's. Looked for
stories about disappearances, about the men Chad had killed in the
HideAway bunkhouse. Knowing no news didn't prove anything.
Knowing she couldn't trust the news.

She avoided e-mail. Last time she'd checked there had been a
message from Mercer, no text, just a video attachment: CCTV footage of her father standing in a hospital gown on a bench surrounded
by tended grass and concrete walks. "Tracks you!" he shouted to doctors walking by. "Paralyzes you at the push of a bureaucrat's *button*."
His hair askew, his feet bare. She'd deleted the video immediately.

Mercer had promised to keep him alive. He'd promised to keep
the others alive too: Krupa, Rajani, Mina. If Catherine played ball.
Said this to her on the shooting deck of the HideAway, speaking
through the distant sound of Chad's gunfire. Told her to compose
herself. Take the podium. Apologize for the disturbance.

So that's what she did. Tried to calm the alarmed reporters. Told
them lies about how she felt, how well Cytofit seemed to work.
Watched the reporters leave.

Late that night: another procedure on the heated table at the

clinic in Gramercy, Sandy Robeson cutting into her again. And then
more lies: "It feels like a miracle, honestly. Like I can finally get on
with my life." She'd said that to a stringer for the *Los Angeles Times*.
She'd spoken to reporters from a hotel room in midtown, where
she stayed for three weeks. "I've never slept so well in my life. With
this thing in me? Sleep like the *dead*." She said that to an editor
at the *Economist*. She'd done all the interviews by phone, flatly re-
fusing to go on TV, so it was Mercer who had sat on the couches
on *Today* and *Good Morning America* to talk about Acetor and its
breakthrough implant. "Life is about to change," he told the beam-
ing hosts, his legs crossed at the knee.

Three weeks was the period she and Mercer had agreed to.
When the three weeks were done, she'd taken a limo to JFK and
picked up her ticket at the Budgetair counter, the only commercial
airline still flying to the second-worst place on Earth.

Why? Because of Frances and Laird. Because it felt like the
farthest she could get from Chad and Mercer. Because Scotland
had barely any government to speak of. Because where else was she
going to go?

67

After the flurry of coverage, Cytofit hadn't remained the top story, but Mercer did seem to be keeping it in the cycle. There'd been a Bloomberg piece about Acetor's fulfilling its first round of Cytofit orders: "Sources say customers are CEOs, Wall Street executives, and investment managers, and Cytofit's price tag is believed to top one million dollars." This morning: a *Wall Street Journal* piece reporting rumors of an Acetor IPO.

The connection cut, and she closed the laptop and went down the wide staircase, past the standing suit of armor, visor lowered, shield tucked close, shoulders draped in a tartan blanket. She had once tried to lift the visor to determine conclusively that there was no one inside, but the metal hinge wouldn't budge. Morning sunlight slid through glassed embrasures in the wall. She paused for a moment in front of one, trying to appreciate the feeble warmth. She closed her eyes and thought of summer; "Summer in Perthshire," Laird had assured her, "is fooking paradise." But this was December, which meant it would be dark by three and Lethendy would turn cold as a tomb.

She heard the front door open and Laird greet the dogs. What time was it? The morning rounds were usually her responsibility; she loved the hushed quiet, loved watching the dogs cut through the mist, chasing hares and grouse, and the men she'd discovered had all been sleepy vagrants with bedrolls and backpacks—not the type to give her any trouble. One or two had begged her for food, but she'd run them off the way Laird had taught her: by ordering the dogs to "scare 'em," a command that would set them barking like lunatics, and by shooting over the mens' heads. Laird had been more seriously challenged, usually in the evenings, by kids with knives who were just settling into impromptu campsites, just opening beers, who were slow to leave, who'd promise to return in greater numbers, with guns, and take the house and everything in it. Laird said not to take them too seriously, and that easier targets existed all over the countryside.

She checked the high shelf at the bottom of the stairs. The twenty-gauge Beretta was missing. She unlatched the heavy front door, a massive thing of thick, steel-braced oak, and stepped out into the chill.

The silky black Labradors that Catherine had named Larry, Curly, and Moe bounded over, their nails clicking on frost-webbed flagstones. They'd come with the property; the owner who'd modernized Lethendy and then abandoned it at the start of the TX outbreak had left them behind. "S'okay, Cathy," Laird said. He wore heavy rubber boots, a turtleneck sweater, and a traditional Barbour jacket—clothes the owner had also left behind. He carried the Beretta broken open on his forearm. His jacket pocket bulged with shotgun shells.

"Sorry—I was just reading the news," Catherine said. "Hello, boys!" All three swished their tails; their tongues pulsed in their mouths.

"Lock was broken by the east gate last night," Laird said. "Better if I go look."

"Mornings are my job," Catherine said, taking a step toward him.

"I'm all dressed. Do the midday round if you like."

So she scratched the dogs' heads, let them lick her hands, and told Laird, in her customary way, to be careful.

In the antique kitchen she saw the food Laird had laid out: powdered eggs, a few carrots, a potato or two, and tinned salmon out of the basement. Big-bellied Frances came downstairs in mean shape, sunken-eyed, underslept, hostile.

She tipped over the stacked salmon cans Laird had arranged next to the sink. "Please tell me we're not eating this cat food today," she said.

"Bad night?" Catherine asked.

She received a scowl in return. "Peed like sixteen times."

This was the way she'd been since Catherine arrived—even before, according to Laird. Catherine had taken to the rugged simplicity of life in Perthshire, the hard work of chopping wood, hand-washing clothes, patrolling the property line, the exhausted dreamless nights each day led to. Not Frances. She'd come excited to be reunited with Laird but had been dismayed by how basic and precarious the existence was. How little there was to do (besides chores) and how uncomfortable pregnancy could be. Lethendy didn't have a TV and Frances didn't have the energy to go out on patrol with Catherine, so she was bored all the time. Cold all the time. Fed up with Laird's bright talk about the future, about being a dad, about the pioneer life they were making for themselves. "It's not even his," she liked to remind Catherine, proudly, as if she were proving something.

Weeks ago Frances had finally told Laird the baby was in fact Mercer's. They had started sleeping in separate bedrooms (Lethendy had seven, so there were plenty to choose from). The relationship seemed to be on hiatus, or possibly over. Frances would lie around in her bed for long portions of the day, and when Catherine came in to see if she wanted anything, if she was okay, Frances would start in about how she'd been making good money with Mercer, how if Catherine hadn't come along and messed things up by throwing herself at him all those months ago, she'd never have wound up in this third-world country . . . Catherine listened as sympathetically as she could. She understood that being eighteen, pregnant, and stuck in the middle-of-nowhere Scotland wasn't everybody's happy ending.

Frances said she had her trust fund, so no one could keep her here. She'd have the baby and then the two of them would give Paris a whirl. Or Rome. Or she'd just go to Connecticut, stick her mom with child care, and Frances could enroll in college somewhere. "Then you and Laird can do what you want," Frances concluded bitterly. Catherine never knew how to respond.

It was no use reminding her about the speech Chad had delivered. About the people he'd killed. Frances had already shrugged all of this information off. Chad wouldn't do anything to her. What would be the point of *that*?

68

Then you and Laird can do what you want.

It had already happened. Late one night after Frances had gone to sleep, Catherine and Laird sat in front of a fire in the hearth and shared a glass of scotch. Laird started describing, as he so often did, what the spring would be like, predicting fresh vegetables and trout in the stream and sun that would actually warm your face. Catherine wished he would stop talking and touch her instead but she didn't want to ask. She leaned into him, shivering, and magically that worked. He put his fingers in her hair, making her head and neck tingle. She laid a hand on his knee, then ran it up under his shirt. They didn't make eye contact, just got undressed quickly, urgently, as if trying not to think twice about what they were doing. Catherine had been struck by how thin and white Laird was, his chest scattered with moles, how clean he smelled and how conscientious he was, entering her slowly, sliding a pillow between her ass and the stone hearth. "Does that hurt?" he'd whispered in her ear. "Cathy?" She'd shushed him, gripped his hips; she couldn't believe it but she was coming—out of nowhere, a wave of pleasure so sudden and acute she'd cried out. Breathing roughly, Laird thrust hard into her, pulled out, and grabbed his trousers to catch his mess.

"My mistake," he said after. Catherine shook her head, still dizzy, still faintly vibrating, like a struck bell.

Then she added: "Not a mistake at all."

"No," Laird said, relieved.

69

Catherine collected the Beretta from her room, put on her coat and rubber boots, and walked down to the empty swimming pool. The dogs yipped and panted, circling her, their breath steaming in the cold, damp air.

Patrolling the grounds centered her. She liked walking the over-grown greens and weedy traps of the nine-hole golf course. She liked testing the sturdy padlocks at each iron gate along the walled boundary. She liked watching the dogs run.

She felt for the scar in her back—uglier and fatter now. She took it on faith that the Cyto was actually out. She took it on faith that Mercer hadn't had Robeson simply insert a newer model while she lay on that heated table. She had no proof, and what would her father say? He was the one talking to her now, a voice falling out of the leaden winter sky.

It's still there, duck. You know it is. You're a dot on Acetor's map.

She picked up her pace and made for the line of alders down by the stream, thinking of Laird's assurances that it would be stuffed with trout come spring. "We'll eat like kings," he liked to say. It was sweet how he said these things to her, constantly assuring her that life here would improve. Laird told her that they would start being more self-sufficient, grow vegetables on the grounds, acquire a few of the sheep they saw dotting the landscape for milk and cheese.

He'd also confided to her that he had no intention of following through on his plan to bring Americans over for shooting holidays. Impending parenthood had changed his whole mind-set. He didn't care if Mercer was the father. He had put a first-class obstetrician in Perth on retainer, and said he had a private hospital room all sorted for the delivery. He was prepared to love that baby as if it were his own. "I'm a new man, Cathy," he'd said to her.

Catherine felt like a new person too. For her, for the first time in her life, one day ended and the next began. She still expected Chad to appear at any moment. Laird wondered why he would, but Laird hadn't heard his speech either. Hadn't seen what he'd done in the bunkhouse.

She scanned the grounds, experiencing an anticipatory charge every time she saw shadows in the trees.

She crossed the flat stones, the dogs splashing along beside her, and climbed the rise of the west field. Over here was the Pictish stone Laird had shown her, on an elevated spot, with a good view of the whole estate. A weather-beaten hulk of gray. Catherine tripped her fingers through the lichen, feeling for the intricate carvings beneath.

Your mind is racing. You're starting to shake. Chad's taunts returned to her as she aimed the Beretta at the horizon, practicing holding her breath and turning still.

Larry bounded up to her, wondering why she was standing there. She looked him in the wet, black eyes and saw only a simple gentleness. *What a sweet, coarse-haired monster*, she thought, and sank her fingers into his thick coat. His brothers barked jealously, piling in. She laughed. "Come on," she said. They scattered east, along her customary route, toward the piebald greens and weedy traps of the course.

The sky was crammed with low clouds; her feet turned to blocks in her rubber boots. She watched the Stooges move across the overgrown fairways.

He's coming, Catherine thought. And felt the cold trigger against her finger. The thought arrived. The sensation. She wanted it. She closed her eyes and felt the steel curve against her trembling finger.

A nice ending.

To her right was a grassy field and a cluster of upright, bulky boulders. Leaning against one was a man, his eyes closed, his rucksack beside him.

She was startled for a moment. She tried to see, from this distance, if the man had any weapons.

He stirred and rubbed his face. He seemed to be waking up. She felt in the coat pocket—a half dozen shells were there. *Two shots*, she reminded herself, then a thumb latch broke the Beretta open. Practicing every day, she'd gotten quick, needing only a few seconds to reload. She thumbed the safety and tightened her grip on the gun.

He'd seen her. He was calling over. She couldn't make out what he was saying. His face was like chalk. A rough beard. Looked like he'd been sleeping outside for days. The rucksack had a bedroll tied to its base.

The first time is hard, she thought. She lifted the gun and aimed low. She nestled her finger into the curve of the Beretta's trigger and leaned into the kick. Her first shot folded the man over, puppetlike. He blinked at his torn jeans. She breathed out, lowered the gun, emptying her head. The gunsmoke tickled her nose. This time, she aimed properly and found that her hands were steady.

ACKNOWLEDGMENTS

Thank you to my early and faithful readers, Callie Wright and Jenny Hollowell. Thank you to DW Gibson and Ledig House where portions of this novel were written. Thank you to Pardis Sabeti, Matt Stremlau, and Aaron Lin for scientific advice. Thank you to my agent Joe Veltre for going the distance with me on this one, and to my editor Lucas Wittmann for his enthusiasm and thoughtful guidance. And above all, thank you to Liz, who lived with this book along with me and whose love and support matters more to me than I can say.